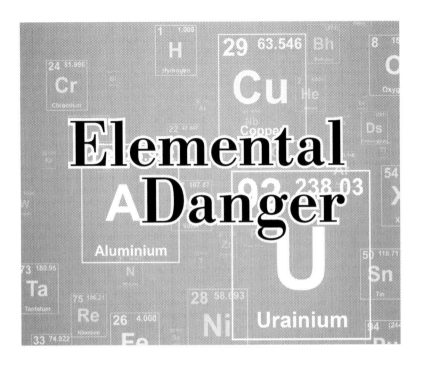

Elemental A Danger

WILLOUGHBY S. HUNDLEY III, MD

iUniverse LLC
Bloomington

ELEMENTAL DANGER

iUniverse books may be ordered through booksellers or by contacting:

iUniverse
1663 Liberty Drive
Bloomington, IN 47403
www.iuniverse.com
1-800-Authors (1-800-288-4677)

ISBN: 978-1-4917-3448-3 (sc)
ISBN: 978-1-4917-3449-0 (hc)
ISBN: 978-1-4917-3447-6 (e)

Library of Congress Control Number: 2014909862

Printed in the United States of America.

iUniverse rev. date: 6/11/2014

My greatest thanks for the support of my family and especially Zadie Beth for her contributions.

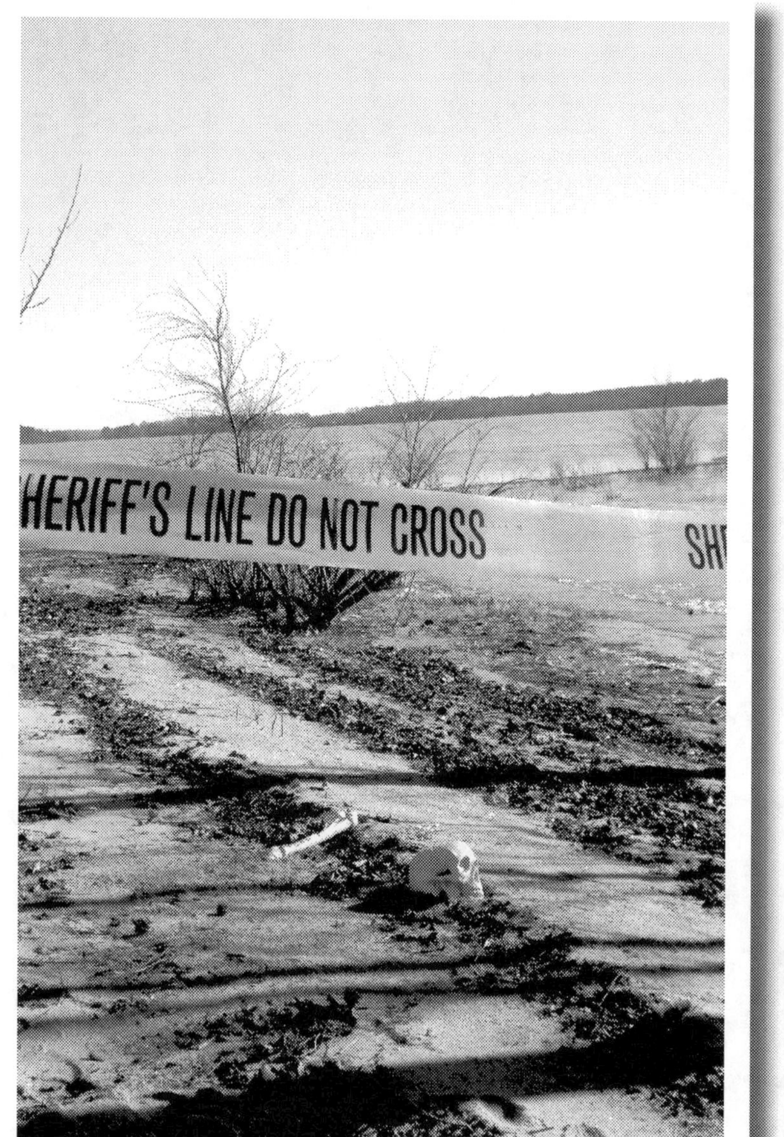
HERIFF'S LINE DO NOT CROSS
SH

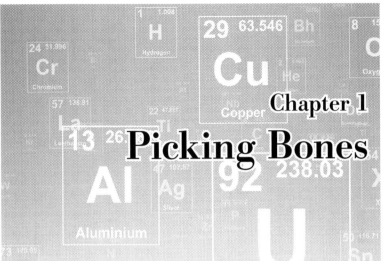

Chapter 1
Picking Bones

It was a pleasant, sunny May afternoon in rural Virginia. Since it was a Wednesday, Dr. Obie Hardy was finishing his office work early, planning to enjoy his yard and grill some hamburgers. For over two decades he had practiced family medicine in the small town of Boydton. As he dropped a final stack of office charts on the refile counter, his medical assistant, Loren, spoke.

"The sheriff's office needs a medical examiner," she said.

"Great," sighed Dr. Hardy.

"They're on line one," she added.

"Dr. Hardy," he said, hitting the speaker phone button. All of his patients were gone for the day, so this discussion would still be private.

"Yes. We need an ME on Route 722, Buffalo Springs area, near the Harrison County line." Dr. Hardy realized this was at least twenty miles one way. A typical death scene visit took him over an hour to work. It might well be dark by the time he got home now. "It's on the lake shore."

"Okay. I'm on my way."

Dr. Hardy was one of the five doctors in Mecklenburg County who served as local medical examiners, or coroners. They worked fatality cases as extensions of the central office into their rural community, a hundred miles from Richmond. Local MEs received a small per case stipend for collecting the necessary information and body fluid specimens, if needed. He grabbed his nylon ME bag, stocked with state forms and collection supplies, and headed west on Highway 58.

The tortuous drive down back roads took him past Buffalo Springs to a somewhat geographically isolated region along the southern banks of Buggs Island Lake. A Mecklenburg County police cruiser parked beside a cabin marked the site for Dr. Hardy.

An overweight, uniformed deputy met Dr. Hardy at the cabin. "All right, Doc. I'll take you from here to the scene. It's a couple hundred yards back this way," he said. He led Hardy along a steep path down from a bluff behind the cabin. The vivid blue water spread out below them, and soft mounds of white clouds rolled slowly through the sky above. There was a bridge visible far down the lake, and Dr. Hardy realized it was the train trestle at Clarksville, at least five miles away.

The path ended on a beach of tan colored sand with four-to eight-foot-tall brushy trees scattered about.

"There's Detective Duffer over there," the deputy said and pointed, sounding a little winded.

"Thanks."

Bruce Duffer was a few years younger than Hardy, probably about fifty. This capable Mecklenburg County detective was seasoned by twenty years of experience. He was about six feet tall, had brown hair, and wore a dress shirt and khakis. He looked over at Hardy.

"Dr. Hardy. We found these remains over here." Hardy approached cautiously, expecting a water-logged corpse, wet and decayed. "The remains are all skeletal," he announced, gesturing toward the wooded area up the beach. "We've marked and photographed the bones up front. You can check those first."

Hardy walked toward the first marker, where he found a large bone. He identified it as a left femur (thigh) bone. He marveled at the pristine condition of the bone, a welcome change from the fetid, rotting bodies often encountered by MEs. Detective Duffer had brought him a large, brown paper bag.

"Left femur," he announced, carefully depositing it into the bag. The bone was white and dry; no adherent organic material remained. The next skeletal element marked was the pelvis. It was completely intact. The osseous ring demonstrated an unmistakably masculine contour. "This is a male," stated Dr. Hardy.

"Are you sure?" asked the overweight deputy, Johnson.

"Yeah," he said. "Definitely."

"Well, there's a female missing person from Harrison County. She's been lost about three months. People said she was kinda manly, not very feminine. Could this be her?"

"No, it's a male pelvis," remarked Hardy. "And, besides, these bones have been here over six months." The sand, sun, and weather had cleaned and bleached this skeleton to the quality of an anatomic teaching model.

"Any idea on how old he was?" asked Duffer. Hardy had just harvested another bone sample, a portion of the lumbar spine. Five vertebrae were fused with calcified, hardened growth connecting them. This was an arthritic process that would not be seen in a young adult.

"Over thirty," stated Hardy. "Probably age fifty to sixty." The osteoporosis seen with more advanced ages was not present. As they proceeded inland to the woods, the bones were more scattered—a couple of hand bones, some ribs, a clavicle, and so on. Dr. Hardy was losing track of which bones had been recovered. He noted Duffer held additional bags. "Bruce, can we sort the bags for different body parts?"

"Sure. How many do you need?"

"Upper extremities, lower extremities, spine and pelvis, ribs and head. Four or five, I guess."

"No problem. Just tell me how you want to label them."

"Okay. We'll put these vertebrae in with the pelvis. Label it 'spine and pelvis.'"

Recovery became more difficult as they entered the edge of the woods. Ribs and long bones blended in with the branches and twigs on the ground, partially buried in the sandy soil and leaves. The time intervals between bone findings grew longer as the daylight waned. Dusk seemed to be falling early.

"We'll have to come back tomorrow," said Detective Duffer. "The storm's almost here."

Dr. Hardy had been engrossed in completing the skeletal puzzle, unaware of the ominous dark clouds approaching. He now realized the wind was whipping up.

"Let's get these bones to the van," Duffer directed. He'd marked the perimeter with yellow police tape and had methodically laid out a grid, plotting the coordinates of each bone. His arduous labor could be eradicated by a heavy storm. Dr. Hardy led the ascent along the path, followed by Deputy Johnson, carrying the bone bags, and lastly Detective Duffer.

The tan van with "Mecklenburg County Crime Scene Unit" painted on it was parked near the cottage. As Duffer placed the bones inside, the first raindrops began falling.

"I noticed," he remarked, "there were no signs of clothing. No shoes, belt buckles, jewelry, or purse fragments. Either this person was nude or was moved from the site of death. You would expect some clothing remnants to remain. You know, zippers, buttons, or something."

"Yeah. I would think so, too," responded Hardy.

"I'll come back tomorrow with a metal detector and sift the sand for trace evidence."

"Okay. I'll send my preliminary report to the Richmond office." The rain began to intensify and the group dispersed to their vehicles. Dr. Hardy called his wife on the drive home and offered to pick up pizza, the backyard barbecue having been spoiled. He could complete the CME-1 form after supper.

"That's fine," replied his wife, Lucy. "I'll make us salads and some tea."

Dinner conversation at the Hardy home often involved medical topics since Lucy was a nurse and his office manager. Their two daughters were accustomed to this.

"So, the body was all bones?" Lucy asked.

"Yeah. Clean as an anatomy model," he stated.

"Neat," responded Anna.

"Yeah," added Vikki, the eldest. "I can't wait to tell Mr. Callahan, my earth science teacher." She was a high school senior, but also a governor's school participant: one of the eight students selected by her high school to spend half of each school day at the local community college. The program earned her college credits for these advanced courses. "Who do you think he was?"

"We don't know yet, but you know I don't mix names and tales!" He was emphatic about this. The rural community was small and healthcare data was privileged information. Occupational stories occasionally surfaced over meals as the family shared their day's events, but people were never identified. "It's still under investigation."

Boydton Life Station was the local rescue squad organization. Dr. Hardy volunteered as the operational medical director, or OMD. He had been urged to attend this week's meeting, as they were desperately seeking to replace their twenty-year-old facility. Alan Hancock, the squad captain, presided over the meeting. He was tall, with reddish brown hair and a mustache.

"Ya'll know we've used this building since 1987 when we started up. Even back then, it was a used double-wide that was graciously donated." With only six initial members, the squad had formed as a satellite of the well-established Chase City squad. Independent after the first two years, it now boasted twelve active members and was experiencing growing pains. "First Citizens Bank has approved a construction loan for us of $480,000. We need to find a contractor and then make plans for a temporary base of operations until the construction is done. Anybody know a good contractor around here?"

"Shouldn't we put it up for bids?" asked Mr. McClain, a black, middle aged squad member.

"I think that would be wise," said Dr. Hardy. "I just got one estimate on my house and it's been a nightmare!" His residential construction was two months over the planned completion date with no definite end in sight. "Be sure to get a deadline with penalties in the contract."

"Who's your contractor, Dr. Hardy?" asked Alan.

"Greg Jackson. He's distant kin, like a step cousin-in-law. Be wary of him."

"So, he's asshole kin, as we say," Alan said wryly.

"Yeah. Exactly!"

"We can run a newspaper ad and get bids," continued Hancock.

"I can get Mark to put it in," said Mr. McClain. His son, Mark McClain, worked as a reporter for *The News Progress*, one of the county newspapers. Mark had volunteered with Boydton Life Station for several years in the past as an EMT—emergency medical technician.

"Great," responded Hancock. "We can put Mark to work, since he don't ride calls with us anymore."

Mr. McClain's son, Mark, was a tall, lanky black man, thirty-six years old. In addition to emergency training, he had studied business and communications at J. Sargent Reynolds Community College in Richmond. When he was asked, he was pleased to write the Boydton Life Station bid request ad for his paper. Indeed, he submitted it as a size upgrade from the category purchased by the squad. It was just a little community service contribution by him. He was also working up a full-page ad layout for the opponents of the ethanol plant in Chase City. This proposed plant was bread-and-butter for the newspaper, as both proponents and antagonists bought ads to air their views.

Obie Hardy drove out to the construction site of his future home to meet with his contractor, Greg Jackson. It was on a secluded wooded lot, one-half mile from the paved road. Although off the beaten path, its saving grace was its lakeside location. Obie noted, as he approached the lot, that the massive columns for the front porch were still lying on the ground. With only pinewood timbers propping up the porch roof, the colonial-style brick house lacked its potential glory. It was but one of the unfinished tasks that Greg's slothering had plagued the project with.

Greg sat on the tailgate of his white pickup truck. He was forty-seven, had black hair peppered with gray, and a mustache. His T-shirt didn't mask his beer-gut torso.

"I thought you said you'd put up the columns last week," began Hardy.

"Well, my helpers quit on me," explained Greg. "I've got ads out for replacements."

"I paid for those columns four months ago! They've just been lying on the ground! I could've saved a lot in interest if you had waited and ordered when you were ready for them."

"Well, the bricklayers didn't work for six weeks. I couldn't put them up until they were finished."

Obie paused. His construction loan interest was costing him $150 per day. The bank had extended the twelve-month construction loan for three months, which would end in four weeks. His mortgage company wouldn't assume the debt until a certificate of occupancy was issued. This festering construction process was rapidly coming to a head.

"When is your expected completion date?" Obie asked, still maintaining his composure.

"I guess another four to six weeks." This was the third month he had given this "four to six weeks" prediction.

"My loan runs out in four weeks. I've already had to get an extension. This is gonna be tight!"

"Oh. Here's the bill for April," added Greg, handing Obie the all-too-familiar manila envelope. Obie sensed Greg was smirking behind his mustache.

"Well, the bank says the next draw will be the final payment. I'll turn this in, but they'll hold it until the 'four to six weeks' completion date." A short silence ensued.

"Do you not want me to work anymore?" asked Greg.

"I just want the job done!" Obie exclaimed. At this point, he didn't care who finished the project.

"All right," agreed Greg.

Obie carried off his manila envelope, walking to the house to survey the progress. Greg pulled a beer out of his cooler to drink on the long drive out to the road and started up his truck.

Chapter 2

Lake Shore

"Sixteen ninety-one over!" The spotter on the race committee boat called out as the Catalina 22 sailed across the finish line. Obie Hardy and Mike Crawford waved back appreciatively.

"Thank you!" answered Obie from the helm of *Second Wind*, his small sailing yacht. They had entered the Governor's Cup Regatta out of Henderson Point, near Townsville, North Carolina. Their Catalina model was not known as a performance racer, landing them in the bottom third of the finishers. "Mike, take the helm. I'll take down the racing genoa."

"Aye-aye, skipper," said Mike as he reached for the tiller.

The genoa, or foresail, provided the main power for this style boat. Not unlike an airplane wing, the sail's shape and aerodynamics determined the performance. Their racing sail was Kevlar, a strong fiber that held its shape and resisted stretching but was textured more like a smooth tarp than a sheet. Obie Hardy lowered the genoa, guiding it into an accordion-like folded pile on the deck. Instead of the rustling sound produced by nylon sails, it made a crinkling sound like a crinoline petticoat as it piled onto the deck. Hardy clipped the everyday nylon sail onto the line and hoisted it.

He called to Crawford, "Pull in the sheet." The wind rustled the jib sail until Mike cleated the sheet line and it swelled taut, filling with wind. The boat gently accelerated, after having lulled when the racing genoa dropped.

Once ashore, they trailered the vessel, parked the trailer, and unhooked it from the Jeep. *Second Wind* would wait, dry docked, until launching Sunday to complete the two-day regatta.

"We did okay," said Hardy at the wheel of his Jeep. "I'm up for the races tomorrow." His boat crew consisted of Mike Crawford, his friend since high school. Mike was six foot two, on the hefty side or, as Obie would say, good "live ballast."

"Yeah. I hope we have good wind," said Mike.

"Yeah. Me too."

They passed a sign that read, "Tungsten Mine Ahead."

"I heard they were re-opening that tungsten mine," said Mike.

"Really? That's neat. What is tungsten, anyway?"

"I'm not sure. Isn't it the stuff in lightbulb filaments or something?"

"Yeah. I think that's right." The thought of locally extracting valuable elements from the earth intrigued him. There was also a quarry on the Virginia side of the lake.

"I've always heard there is gold in the lake area," added Mike.

"I wouldn't doubt it. I wonder how one would find it?"

"I don't know."

As they drove across the Clarksville Bridge, the columns of the new bridge construction were visible, rising up from the water like the rock pillars of Stonehenge. The lake's surface shimmered in the late afternoon sun. Obie looked westward but was unable to see the distant beach where he had sorted the bones just a month before. He realized he hadn't yet received the final autopsy report from Richmond.

"The water's view will be changed forever when the bypass is completed," Obie remarked.

"Yep. At least the bridge is tall enough for sailboats," added Mike.

"Yeah. It might make sailing underneath it interesting." The currents in the main channel already made steering tricky near the old bridge. Only the future would tell.

Monday, Dr. Hardy saw a patient, Ted Grayson, from the Clarksville area. He was undergoing treatment for blood pressure and cholesterol.

"Do you exercise, Mr. Grayson?" asked Hardy.

"Well," he said, chuckling, "I'm sort of working now."

"Working?" asked Hardy. Ted's chart listed his age as seventy-eight.

"Yeah. I'm consulting on the bypass bridge project." He had a twinkle in his blue eyes. "You see, I'm a geologist. I came here when they built the Rudd's Creek Bridge and decided to retire and stay here." He produced a cylinder of greenish-gray rock from his pocket. "I examine the drill cores, like this one. I work with the engineers to establish loads for the pylons."

"That sounds neat. It hasn't helped your cholesterol, though. The triglycerides have gone up."

He laughed again. "Well, there's not much to do while they drill. I munch a lot—nabs, peanuts, chips. I can cut that out."

"Okay, but if your levels don't come down, we'll increase your medicines."

"Okay, Doc."

"Oh, I was wondering. Since you're a geologist, do you know if there's any gold in the area?"

"I've heard people talk about it, but none to speak of. Mostly fool's gold, or pyrite."

"There's so much rock on my new homesite, I've wondered if I could open a quarry."

"I have a geological map of the state. I could get you one, if you'd like."

"Really? I'd love one."

"Okay."

"Thanks. And in three months we'll repeat your labs."

Robert Meadows was another patient in for a routine visit that week. His health problems entailed diabetes and high cholesterol, inconvenient for a large man who enjoyed eating. Being an outdoorsman was somewhat of a saving grace, as golfing and hunting afforded him some year-round activities—an informal exercise program. He worked for the Army Corps of Engineers, the organization that managed the lake reservoir.

"Anything new with the corps?" asked Dr. Hardy, as he looked over the home blood sugar readings.

"Well, I'm helping some with the archeological dig. That's interesting."

"Archeological dig? What's that?"

"It seems the corps realized they didn't have enough historical and environmental information on the river basin forming the lake—past vegetation flora, Native American inhabitation, et cetera. They were some limited funds available to them to conduct a study."

"I hadn't heard about that."

"Well, it's secretive. They don't want spectators around, disturbing or vandalizing the site, searching for artifacts or gold."

"Wow! That's fascinating! My daughter's taking geology in governor's school and will love hearing about this. A dig in Mecklenburg County!"

They discussed his diabetic readings and his weight, which was down slightly. "The Vytorin injections have improved your diabetes. We still need to work on your cholesterol and triglycerides. I think we need to add another lipid-lowering drug."

"Let's just hold off for now, Doc. I'll work harder on my diet and weight. Can we re-check it next visit?" asked Mr. Meadows.

"Well, all right. But you'll need to return in three months."

The following day, Dr. Hardy had all but forgotten about the dig when Mr. Meadows called him at work.

"Dr. Hardy, I talked with our archeological team today. If you're interested, I can take you and your daughter to the dig site, but you absolutely *cannot* tell *anyone* about the location!"

"No problem. That's great! When can we go there?"

"Maybe Thursday morning. There are a lot of people around on the weekends."

"All right! I can make that work." It was June, and Vikki was out of school for the summer. He could get Dr. Richards to make hospital rounds for him that morning.

"Okay. I'll call you the day before with directions."

"Great. Thanks so much!" The covert nature of their plan gave it a bit of an Indiana Jones feeling. Dr. Hardy anxiously anticipated their encounter.

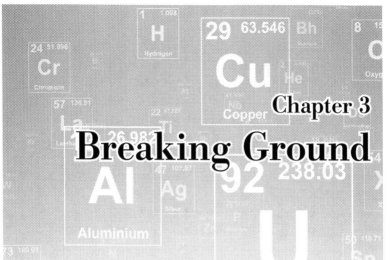

Chapter 3
Breaking Ground

L ocal reporter Mark McClain sat at his computer studying satellite images of the area around Chase City. He wanted a photo for his article that showed the proposed ethanol plant's proximity to the town. The site was only a mile and a half from town center, where the two highways intersected. This was glaringly evident in the aerial view he just selected.

"Bingo!" he said. "This is it." He was preparing an article to run the week of the town meeting being held to discuss this potential industry. The local news usually focused on high school athletics or the week's largest fish caught in Buggs Island Lake. This controversial developing issue excited him. The community was divided on the issue, weighing new jobs and agricultural production against the stench of the fermenting mash byproduct that would amass. Tobacco, the historical money crop of the area, had been smothered by contracting and regulations. Virginia's fine tobacco was recognized worldwide. However, the quality of Mexican tobacco had greatly improved, thanks to migrant workers carrying Virginia's technology home. Corn harvesting would provide a basis for the mash, hence alcohol production would replace nicotine—a drug for a drug, so to speak. Mark had yet to choose sides, maintaining his objectivity, but leaned in favor of the plant. He felt that the long-term benefits of jobs, crop demands, and economic growth outweighed the risks. Besides, if significant problems were created, the plant could always be shut down. He planned to let the upcoming meeting sway his allegiance.

The Robert E. Lee Building was three-quarters filled with local residents longing to voice their opinions and debate over the Chase City ethanol plant project. Mark McClain had arrived early, prepared to ingest the entire event. He had brought his digital camera, microrecorder, and notepad. Among the many faces were familiar citizens and community leaders, including the Chase City town manager, members of the county board of supervisors, and area agricultural agents. Probably the most prominent of these was Sidney Francis, a state senator. Rural Virginia was fortunate to have a legislator with roots in the community. Mark snapped a photo of Sidney talking with members of the board of supervisors.

A voice rang out over the PA system. "Could I have your attention, please? If we could all find a seat, we'll get this thing started." The speaker was a plump, middle-aged man with sandy-colored hair and a mustache. He paused for the crowd to settle. "You may know me. I'm Ralph Riggins, the mayor of Chase City. We'll begin our forum on the ethanol plant proposal with a statement from the company, Bios Power Alternatives. Questions will be fielded afterward, and then the floor will be open for anyone to speak. The sign-up sheet is down here. If you'd like to speak and you're not signed up yet, please add your name to the list.

"Now, without further ado, I present to you Kelly Dalton, marketing executive for BPA."

"Thank you, Mayor Riggins. As you said, I represent Bios Power Alternatives and I'm, so to speak, the Indian scout. I'm supposed to provide information and answers concerning our proposed ethanol generation plant. We have three other plant locations already in Virginia and North Carolina. These communities have embraced our industry and we've become good neighbors. We would hope to enjoy a similar relationship here." He was a blond man in his mid-thirties in typical business attire: a navy suit and a tie. His presentation heralded the obvious benefits of jobs and the environmental assets of a biogenetic fuel component. "Just one of our facilities generated $2 million in local tax revenues in 2006." Mayor Riggins's eyebrows shot up at hearing that figure. Such money would be a godsend to a small town. "You may be aware that the federal government has mandated that, by 2014, 20 percent of fuels must be from renewable sources. In other words, not from fossil sources such as coal, oil, or gas."

Mark McClain was impressed by the BPA executive's speech, but was still aware that this was what he was paid to do—not exactly unbiased. Harold Edwards led off the community speakers. He appeared to be in his late fifties, wore glasses, and was balding.

"I'm with the Association to Preserve Mecklenburg. We strive to protect our precious county from potential threats. We have strong concerns over the repercussions of such an industry as yours.

"Number one: air pollution produced from the distillery furnace.

"Number two: the smell of the fermented mash. A similar site in Hopkinsville, Kentucky, reported a sour smell noted up to a mile away. We're all too familiar with paper mills and chicken farms already.

"Number three: increased truck traffic. This will bring more highway maintenance costs, congestion, and noise.

"Number four: sewage runoff. There's always a risk of contaminating our lake reservoir. Mecklenburg County's greatest assets are environmental. We have fresh air, clean water, and rich fields and woods. The bottom line on ethanol plants is if you don't have one, you don't need one!"

Mark made some notes. He was familiar with the Association to Preserve Mecklenburg from their newspaper ads. The next speaker was a stranger to him. She was tall, maybe five nine, brunette, and in her late thirties. Mark was immediately drawn to her. Her skin was olive toned, an international look, hinting of Native American heritage or a cultured blend.

"I'm Vanessa Foster. I teach communications at Southside Virginia Community Colleges. I'm as concerned over our environment as anyone. When you consider the alternative energy sources, ethanol is the least toxic. We've all seen the smog haze over our large cities. Do you remember the Chernobyl plant radiation leak in 1986? Or the Three Mile Island meltdown? The Valdez oil spill in 1989? Even our most recent Gulf Oil spill? Oil spills are an almost annual event worldwide. There have been twenty-four spills between 1988 and 2008, with an average of about 4 million gallons of crude oil each, soiling our planet. I think the ethanol plant should be here, for our economy now and for our children's future. Thank you."

Mark McClain was so engrossed with the speaker that he had neglected to photograph her. He made a rushed attempt to get a shot as she walked off. Dissatisfied with his photo, he made his way toward her. The camera and notepad exposed his profession as he approached her.

"Ms. Foster," he called.

"Yes?" she answered, smiling. "Are you a reporter?"

"Yes, ma'am. Mark McClain, *The News Progress*." She was quite striking up close. Her skirt and blouse were crisp, setting off her well-proportioned figure. Mark wished he had more of a pick-up line. "Can I get a picture of you for the paper?"

"Only if you lose the 'ma'am', Mr. McClain. It's Vanessa." She smiled.

"Yes, ma'am—I mean, great!" He nervously clicked a few shots from different angles.

"Do I get a copy of the proofs?" she asked teasingly.

"Sure. No problem. I'll need—"

"My address?" She took his notepad and pen and began writing. "E-mail me here."

"Yes, ma— er, absolutely." The ethanol plant forum assignment had paid off for Mark. The debate now drew his undivided attention. His stance on the controversy was now solidly rooted in favor of the plant.

Day was just breaking as Dr. Hardy and Vikki turned into the boat launch area just below the dam. Mr. Meadows had already arrived and launched an aluminum john boat, secured to the bank by a nylon rope. As the water flowed by, a fog rose from it's surface.

Meadows greeted them as they got out of the Jeep. "Dr. Hardy, glad you could come."

"I wouldn't miss it. Mr. Meadows, this is Vikki."

"Hello, Vikki. I've got a present for you." He handed her an orange life jacket.

"Gee, thanks," she answered sarcastically.

"Both of you," Meadows said, extending another jacket to Dr. Hardy. "Hop in and we'll ride over."

The gentle rumbling of the river was interrupted by the drone of the small outboard motor. The mist that emanated from the water condensed into fine droplets on Dr. Hardy's forearms. Their route took several turns along a serpentine course.

"This is in case someone saw which direction we were headed in," explained Mr. Meadows. Hardy noted that the visibility was only about fifty feet in the fog and felt that these maneuvers might be unnecessary. Then, finally, an island emerged from the cloudy veil, and they beached their ferry.

Robert Meadows led the party up from the shore and down a path where two men were digging with garden tools. He introduced Dr. Hardy and Vikki to the archeologists. The elder man took the lead and began briefing them on the excavation. He was slender and his tanned skin accentuated the thick white hair receding from his brow. His eyes twinkled, sparked by an audience interested in his work.

"We use the layers of pollen to estimate the age of artifacts that we uncover," he explained. "We have reached down to the 1500s in a few spots here."

Hardy realized that was in Columbus's era.

"What about carbon dating?" asked Vikki. "They've talked about that in science class. Do you use that?"

"Well, it's more high tech. It's based on the carbon-14 isotope of normal carbon-12. Living systems are in equilibrium with the tiny concentrations of C-14 in the atmosphere. Once they die, they cease to breathe and exchange carbon with their environment. The slow breakdown or loss of C-14 can be plotted to track the age of the fossil. The half-life of C-14 is over five thousand years."

"That's neat!"

"Well, it involves measuring radioisotopes. That has to be done in special labs."

"What things have you found around here?" asked Dr. Hardy. "Any arrowheads?"

"They're called 'projectile points' now," explained Meadows. "That covers arrowheads and spears."

"A few," answered the archeologist. "Some pottery fragments. As a matter of fact, we're working on what looks to be a bowl now." He led them to the edge of the digging ditch. There was a rounded, bulging object protruding from the soil. "It's very fragile, so our work is slow and tedious." He pointed to some jagged markings on the surface. "It's odd to see these worm or insect borings along the surface."

Dr. Hardy and Vikki took a closer look. Something appeared familiar to the physician. "Worm trails or cranial sutures?" he asked.

"Cranial sutures?" the archeologist responded. He seemed moved by the sudden realization that the bowl could actually be a skull. "My God! You may be right!"

"It's funny," said Hardy. "We found skeletal remains about two months ago fifteen miles upstream. They weren't this old, though."

"These could be a hundred to a hundred fifty years old, partially fossilized."

"Is it an Indian?" asked Vikki.

"Quite possibly. We'll need an anthropologist to make that call. And carbon dating might be used here."

"Awesome!" squealed Vikki.

"There was a large Confederate camp near Boydton during the Civil War," stated Meadows. "They crossed the river there at Taylor's Ferry. It could be one of their casualties as well."

"More historical than medical legal," stated Dr. Hardy, from his coroner perspective. "I guess you'll still have to notify the police."

"Oh, definitely," added Meadows. The archeologist appeared concerned. "Don't worry. Be assured that I'll have them keep the dig site location confidential."

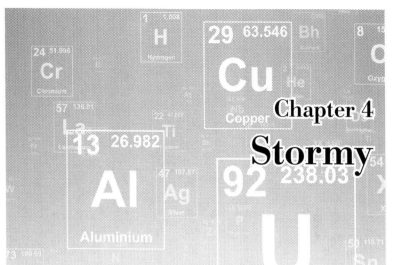

Chapter 4

Stormy

Virginia county MEs served as local agents for the office of the chief medical examiner. Mecklenburg County fell in the territory embraced by the central office in Richmond, with another three regional offices covering remaining areas of the commonwealth. Dr. Hardy had been an agent for the central office for over twenty years. He was accustomed to the six-to-eight-week delay before receiving final autopsy reports on his cases. The archeological dig discovery had reminded him that he had not heard back on the analysis of the beached bones from three months earlier. Curiously, he placed a call to the Richmond office.

"Dr. Downing here. Dr. Hardy?"

"Yes. I'm calling to follow up on a case from Mecklenburg County. It was on skeletal remains. I was hoping to get some information back."

"Oh. The old Indian skull?"

"Well, not really. But I did see the dig site where they found a skull. Was it really an Indian?"

"Probably Native American, yes. We've sent it to the Virginia Museum here. They may have the Smithsonian check it."

"All right! The Occaneechi tribe was prominent here."

"Yes. Related to the Saponi Nation. They'll research it further for confirmation."

"Great! The case I actually called about was the bony remains in the Buffalo Springs area in May. Any progress?"

"Funny you should ask. We had a case posted on a man with prostate cancer who had a recent radiation seed implantation. To determine if it was safe to work it, we brought in a Geiger counter. After using it, we placed it in the store room and it began chirping. Those bones you sent us were lying beside it in the store room. The bottom line is that there was mild to moderate radioactivity found in those bones."

"No kidding? Are we in any danger from our exposure?"

"Not likely. But it's still a mystery as to what's going on. There wasn't any useful DNA. We don't know if he had any occupational exposure. And they're no nuclear facilities near there."

"That's odd."

"Well, it's still under investigation. I'll keep you updated if we find anything."

"Thanks."

That evening, a summer storm arose around dusk. Dark swells of clouds blotted out the orange glow from the setting sun. The utter blackness outside the Hardy home was pierced by bright flashes of lightning in strobed pulses. The shutters slapped the outside walls from the gusts of wind as the lights flickered inside, almost as if they were candles in a breeze. Fortunately, supper had just ended when the blinking lights went out completely. In his blackened kitchen, Obie Hardy welcomed Lucy's infatuation with candles, a trait he usually just tolerated. Within minutes, she had at least one candle lit in each room, although their weak glow was a pale ember against the raging storm.

"Bath time," announced Lucy. The hot water heater was full, and with the electrical outage time unknown, she knew the hottest bath might be now. "Girls, ration the hot water. We don't know how much we'll have." Vikki would certainly not waste a drop. In fact, she would sometimes skip a bath if her mood was so. Anna, however, was known for her long, hot showers. With no electronics or Internet, the teenagers didn't complain about this unscheduled imposition.

By bedtime, the storm had subsided to a mere distant rumbling, and at three thirty in the morning the lights came on, startling Dr. Hardy awake. He wearily reset his alarm clock, turned off the lights, and returned to bed. At five thirty, the phone ringing interrupted his sleep again.

"This is the medical examiner's office. Is Dr. Hardy in?"

"Yeah. Dr. Hardy here," he answered sleepily.

"Can you do a viewing at South Hill Hospital this morning?"

"Yeah, sure. I can do it during rounds."

"The body's in the morgue. Gary Rainer, a lightning strike victim."

"Okay, sure. I'll do it."

After hospital rounds, Dr. Hardy picked up the morgue key from the nurses' station and gathered syringes and test tubes for postmortem body fluid samples. On the basement level, he unlocked the morgue room door to access the six-foottall stainless steel storage unit. The middle shelf held a body, refrigerated and sealed in the white vinyl body bag. The name tag on the zipper read "Gary Rainer," Hardy's assigned case. The copied medical record left with the body listed his age as twenty-three.

Unzipping the bag revealed the face of a young black male. A film of dewy condensation coated the inside of the bag. The moisture intensified the smell of burned hair and flesh. Hardy noted an ulcer on the right side of the neck, surrounded by blackened skin discoloration. The lower border of the discoloration had a feathered appearance, a commonly reported finding in victims of lightning strike injuries. Confident that this represented the entry wound, Hardy turned his attention to the feet. The anklet socks had three small burned areas on the outer edges and over one big toe. He removed Gary's socks to find blackened skin beneath the socks' scorch marks. These external findings indicated that electrocution was the mechanism of death.

To complete his examination, Dr. Hardy log-rolled the body onto the left side. Gary Rainer's entire back was reddened with blistered skin shedding in rippled waves. His tank top looked like it had been pulled out from a fire. The waistband of his underwear was charred. Hardy's earlier findings had shown evidence of a fatal injury. This now revealed that Gary had been literally fried by the lightning strike.

This was Dr. Hardy's first lightning fatality case. A person's lifetime risk of being struck by lightning is about one in three thousand. In rural Mecklenburg County, the population was about forty-three thousand. This would translate into about fourteen strikes per lifetime, or about one every four years. Some lightning strike victims survive, despite this massive power surge averaging one billion volts. Hence, the rarity of such cases would not be unusual.

From reviewing the medical record, Dr. Hardy learned that this young man got out of the car during the storm to urinate. His cousin had watched from inside the vehicle as Gary was struck down. The cousin dragged him into the car and called 9-1-1. It was ten minutes after the injury when the EMS ambulance met them en route to the hospital. Gary did not respond to the EMS resuscitation efforts and was pronounced dead upon arrival to the ER. Dr. Hardy collected a blood sample for the central office, zipped up the vinyl bag, and returned the body to the cooler.

Near closing time at Dr. Hardy's office, the rescue squad captain, Alan Hancock, dropped by. His visits were less of a disruption to the office schedule at this time of day.

"Hardy, did you feel that earthquake last night?" he asked.

"No, but I heard something about it on the radio. Was it around midnight?"

"Yeah. Me and my ole lady were in the sack. I asked her if she felt the earth move. No such luck."

"Well, we can dream," said Dr. Hardy.

"Oh, we got our building permit today. We'll break ground in two weeks."

"That's great!" Dr. Hardy responded.

"We'd like you to be at the groundbreaking ceremony, if you can."

"Why, sure. I'd love to. When?"

"A week from Wednesday, ten in the morning."

"All right. I'll adjust my schedule. I'm not going to have to speak, am I?"

"No. Not unless you want to. The mayor will be there."

"Enough said." Politicians always had a statement if news media were near.

"Oh. You didn't ask me about our contractor." He baited the doctor.

"No. Who did you get?"

Alan paused dramatically. He had received a prior warning from Dr. Hardy. "We got three estimates and the squad picked the lowest at $478,000. Greg Jackson."

"Greg Jackson? Oh, no! Not him!"

"Well, he'll save us at least twenty to thirty thousand."

"Maybe. I hope he does you better than he's done me!"

"Yeah. Me too, Doc."

As scheduled, Dr. Hardy was on location on the Wednesday of the rescue squad groundbreaking. The town mayor joined Alan Hancock and Greg Jackson, all posed holding their ceremonial shovels. The mayor was dressed in a dark suit and tie, Alan in his white rescue squad dress shirt with shoulder rank bars. Mark McClain was among the three photographers who recorded the ceremony. Dr. Hardy stood in the background with the other rescue squad officers, the county sheriff, and some town council members. Behind the group, a bright yellow sign read No Ethanol Plant.

"The town is proud to have this upgraded facility to help meet the emergency-care needs of our community," the mayor said, ever so politically. Dr. Hardy noted that there were more officials than spectators at the event.

As the gathering was dissipating, Dr. Hardy cornered Greg Jackson. "I hope this job doesn't delay the house job anymore."

"Oh, no," Greg said firmly. "This will all be subcontracted. We're almost done with your house anyway. Probably about four to six weeks."

Hardy just shook his head and walked off. He didn't want to dampen the grand spirit of the occasion. Anyway, his office work would, no doubt, be back-logged by now from his absence.

Later that week, Mark McClain was at *The News Progress* office working on some ad layouts. One disadvantage of having a Monday edition newspaper was it went to print on Saturday. It was late August, so the Friday high school football game obligation wasn't haunting him yet. It was not unusual for him to stay at the office to well after closing on Fridays. He was genuinely surprised to have a visitor arrive just minutes before closing.

"Mr. McClain," said Vanessa Foster. "I never got my photos."

Mark felt sheepish. He had found himself looking over her pictures frequently but had procrastinated on sending them. This was partly due to work but, more likely, due to a sense of loyalty to his current girlfriend, Yvonne. Something about Vanessa aroused him, and he couldn't decide whether to fan the flames or keep her at a distance.

"Well, I'm sorry. I was meaning to send them," he began. "I just got distracted with work. In fact, I was going to do it this weekend."

"Uh-huh. I'm sure you were," Vanessa replied.

"Okay, well, I've got them here on my laptop. You can check them out." Mark fumbled with the keyboard. "Did you come here just to get your pictures?"

"Well, I was on my way to Wal-Mart and I thought I might check up on you."

"Here you go," announced Mark, as the screen filled with postage-stamp-sized pictures. "These are yours." He clicked on a photo and it grew to fill the screen.

Vanessa leaned over to study the images. Mark noted her long legs, dressed in black pants that fit snuggly over her rear end. The rounded contour of her buttocks was alluring. He could smell her perfume as he reached to adjust the mouse pad for displaying other photos.

"Not bad," she concluded.

No, not bad at all, Mark thought to himself. "Thanks," he said.

"So, how late do you work Fridays?" she asked, as she reached down and began typing on his keyboard.

Mark scrutinized her actions with his computer. She was attaching the photos to an e-mail. "It depends on how much I have to do. Sometimes till after midnight."

"There! All sent," she said. "One less thing for you to do."

"Thanks," he responded.

"Do you stop to eat?"

"Well, not always." He often became engrossed in his work. His lean physique attested to the fact that he was not a slave to meals. He glanced at his watch and saw it was nearly six o'clock. "Would you like to grab something... to eat?"

"Sure," she said, smiling.

Mark took her to Kahill's, a local restaurant and bar. They picked at their salads and sipped their wine.

"You look great tonight," Mark finally admitted.

"Thanks. You don't look half bad yourself."

"So. How's your work at the community college?"

"It's part-time. Business communications. I only have two classes each semester."

"Does that keep you busy?"

"Well, I do some consulting work for a few businesses, too."

"So, are you married?" Mark probed bluntly.

She laughed. "No! Are you?"

"No." He paused before adding, "I have been seeing someone though."

"Oh." She took a sip of wine. "Is it serious?"

"I don't know." He looked into her eyes and smiled. "Two weeks ago I would have said yes."

"And what's happened to change that?" Vanessa queried.

"You."

Dinner stretched out for an hour and a half. Standing beside their cars in the parking lot, Mark faced Vanessa, uncertain of his next move.

"Thanks for dinner and the company," Vanessa said. She then leaned over and gave him a quick kiss of gratitude. After a brief pause, Mark, with his growing passion, took her in his arms and returned her kiss. He wanted her to stay, but he still had unfinished work at the office and he wanted to keep this respectable.

"Do you like high school football?" asked Mark.

"I guess so. Why?"

"I'm covering the opening game next Friday. I'd like it if you could meet me there."

"Okay. It sounds good! I'll check my schedule."

As Mark got in his car as his cell phone beeped with a text message. It was from Yvonne: "R U still at work?"

He texted a reply. "Yeah. Probably 4 a while." She was a CNA and would be working the night shift at the nursing home. He would just have to deal with her later.

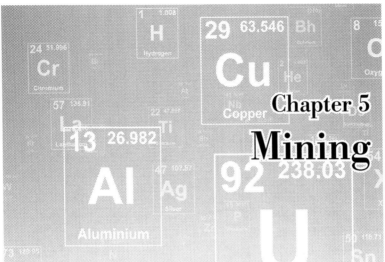

Chapter 5

Mining

Vanessa Foster made a morning drive west along Highway 460 from her Farmville apartment to Roanoke. She had a ten o'clock appointment scheduled with the regional manager of Dixie Prospecting Company. The company had contacted her through her job at the Keysville campus of SVCC and invited her for an interview regarding a work project. Her curiosity was aroused by the possibility of further utilizing her business communications degree. Teaching at SVCC was only a part-time position, so an opportunity to supplement her income was equally appealing.

"Ms. Foster, Mr. Snelling can see you now," announced the secretary.

"Thanks," answered Vanessa. She stood, smoothed out her skirt, and carried her résumé into Mr. Snelling's office. The room boasted a large, elegant oak desk in the center and floor-to-ceiling glass windows behind.

Walter Snelling was a stout man in his mid-forties with a mustache and a balding scalp. He wore a gray business suit and a Cheshire grin.

"Ms. Foster, I'm Walter Snelling and this is Neal Hooker from marketing." He motioned toward a tall black man to his right. Vanessa greeted them and sat in front of the desk. "Mr. Hooker was impressed by your presentation in Chase City at the ethanol plant forum. We have been looking for someone with your capabilities in Southside Virginia."

Vanessa had done her homework. She knew that Dixie Prospecting Company, known as DP, managed several mining operations in Virginia and North Carolina. They also owned a large tract in Harrison County that contained uranium stores. She was unsure as to the environmental safety of uranium mining, so she cautiously withheld her judgment on the issue.

"We hope one day to pursue uranium mining in Virginia," stated Mr. Hooker. "Sadly, the idea instills fear in surrounding communities."

"Virginia has had a moratorium banning uranium mining since 1982," added Mr. Snelling. "They are currently reviewing lifting this ban in the next few years."

"We have launched a public relations and educational campaign, if you please, that focuses on showing the safety of such mining as currently as 2010," continued Mr. Hooker.

"And you think I can help with this?" asked Vanessa, a bit skeptical.

"Well, yes, we do," Snelling said. "We need someone to help with local advertising, attend community functions, and just 'feel out' the area's views, so to speak. We don't want to come across as a greedy, careless industry out to desecrate the environment."

"I see," said Vanessa as she digested the proposal. "How much work would this involve?"

"Well, we would pay you a monthly stipend, say $1,500. You would run local newspaper ads at least once a month and report to us on other local developments and opinions."

"Okay. Say I agree. How long am I committed for?"

"We will offer you a six-month contract, but you may resign at any monthly interval."

"All right," she said. "I'll strongly consider it. When do you need to know?"

"I'll send you a proposal. You can let us know in two weeks or so."

"Okay," she said. She stood up and shook their hands.

As she walked out, Snelling watched her and then turned to Hooker. "What do you think?"

"I think she's perfect for what we need."

"Me, too." The executives shared smiles. "She's smart, attractive, and could create quite a formidable distraction."

John H. Daniel was the name of the Keysville campus of the two area community colleges known as Southside Virginia Community Colleges, SVCC. This campus was host to the governor's school program for selected, accelerated high school students. James Callahan enjoyed teaching science at SVCC, and his passion was reflected most in the governor's school participants. These students were drawn by his enthusiasm to participate in his experiments. He managed to evoke their curiosity and channel their energy into learning experiences.

James Callahan was medium height with sandy-brown, curly hair. He stood in the front of the science classroom in a short-sleeved dress shirt accented with a blue bow tie. The desks were black-topped work benches that seated four students each. The room doubled as the lab and was equipped with sinks and gas supply lines. Behind Callahan were a dry erase board and the periodic table of elements. This was the second week of his Science 101.

"Okay, class," he began. "This is our first lab session. We will be studying a noble gas." He pointed to element 86 on the periodic table. "Radon. Anyone heard of it?"

"Yeah. It's in basements. Right?" responded Andy Francis, the son of Senator Francis.

"You're right, Andy. It seeps out from the ground and, especially from rocks. It's one of the so-called noble gases. The noble gases all share four characteristics: they exist as a monatomic gas in their native state; they are colorless; they are odorless; and they have low chemical reactivity.

"Our concern with radon is that it has radioactivity and, when inhaled, can lead to lung cancer. Today's lab will involve each of you obtaining radon readings from your basements, garages, or crawl spaces under your homes. We will compile the data after three weeks and plot the results by depth of readings and by geographic regions on a state map."

After class, the students were charged up, carrying their radon kits down the hallway. One boy spoke to Andy.

"I don't know about ray-don." He then squeezed out an audible fart. "But 'rip-one' can be a noble gas, too!"

"Aw! That's gross, Keith!" Andy retorted as he quickly stepped away from him. "That's not a noble gas! That's a noxious gas!"

Ted Grayson, the geologist, returned to Dr. Hardy's office for his repeat cholesterol reading. His triglycerides had fallen to 180. He sat in the exam room holding a four-foot-long cardboard cylinder.

"You've done well," said Dr. Hardy. "I think if you added some fish oil or flax seed oil you can get these triglycerides down to our goal."

"Okay. That's easy enough."

"What's with the long tube?" asked Dr. Hardy.

"Oh. It's the state geological map that I got for you." He handed the cardboard tube to the doctor. Dr. Hardy couldn't resist pulling the rolled-up map out of its holder. He unrolled it on the exam table, revealing the state of Virginia subdivided by irregular shapes like a paint-by-number canvas. "Here's the key," said Grayson, pointing to the upper right corner. "It tells the predominant stone type in the marked regions. Sorry, they're no gold deposits in our county."

"This is great!" exclaimed Hardy. "I can't wait to get this home and study it. Thanks! Can I pay you for this?"

"Oh, no! I've got plenty of these! I hope you can enjoy it."

"Absolutely! Thanks a lot."

Alan Hancock stopped by the office about closing time, as he would do occasionally. Dr. Hardy was more receptive to rescue squad updates then, since his patient schedule was not interrupted.

"Doc, have you seen the work on our building?"

"Well, yeah." Hardy had seen that the cement flooring had been poured and the steel framing started. "Is it on schedule so far?"

"Well, it was, but … we had some vandalism," Alan said.

"Vandalism? What happened?"

"Seems there's a wave of robberies in the area involving electrical wire and plumbing."

"That's strange," replied Hardy.

"Not really. The thing is, they take the copper. Metal salvage places are paying four dollars a pound. Thieves are hitting construction sites and ripping out wires and copper pipes. You may want to watch out at your new homesite."

"Well, we lock the doors now that it's near completion. We should be finished in four to six weeks." He mused, sarcastically at this familiar deadline.

"Good. We only lost a couple of rolls of wire, probably less than a week's delay."

"That's good. I guess in the twenty-first century we mine copper a little differently from in the past."

"Yeah. That's one way to look at it."

At home, Dr. Hardy was greeted by Vikki, who was bubbling with excitement.

"Dad! We're going to test our basement for radon for our science project! Isn't that cool?" She held up the test kit box as proof.

"Yeah, sure! That sounds neat!" answered Hardy.

"And next week we're going to see a mine near Townsville!"

"The tungsten mine?" he asked.

"Yeah! Mr. Callahan is the coolest teacher!" She spun around and skipped off to the den. Obie Hardy smiled. He was pleased with her academic performance and the caliber of the governor's school program. He hoped her younger sister, Anna, would be accepted for the upcoming year.

Vanessa had called Mark McClain with a tip about the class trip to the mine in Townsville. She had said it might make a good community interest story. Mark was intrigued and was already on site when the school bus arrived. Vanessa arriving with the group was not a surprise. She had volunteered to accompany James Callahan and assist with the students.

"Mark's with *The News Progress*," she said to Callahan. "We thought a little publicity might help with our governor's school program funding."

"Oh yeah. We can use all the help we can get. Some high schools are only able to sponsor four students a year now," said James Callahan.

They assembled in a small meeting room in the building closest to the mine entrance. The Dixie Prospecting site manager gave them an overview of tungsten mining.

"Tungsten is a metal element, also known as Wolfram, hence its symbol 'W.' Its commercial value lies in its physical properties. It has a melting point of 3,422 degrees centigrade, the second highest of all the elements, making it stable for use in hot environments. That's why it's famous for its use in lightbulb filaments. Tungsten has an extremely high conductivity as well, good for electrical contacts and wires. Its retail value skyrocketed with the electronics boom, which led to the reopening of this mine."

Mark was still making notes as they moved outside. The entrance to the mine itself resembled a traffic tunnel. Centrally, a well-packed dirt roadway trailed off down the incline. There were two four-wheeler ATV vehicles parked on one side with an array of trailer carts. The ATVs were plugged into outlets fed by a network of electrical conduits visible along the wall.

"All our work vehicles are electric," continued the site manager. "Exhaust fumes would be toxic in this enclosed area. You can see our ventilation ducts overhead that circulate air into the deep levels."

Vanessa was standing near Mark behind the students. She leaned toward him and whispered, "I've got to find a restroom."

"Oh, okay," Mark said as he turned to look about the mine. He spotted some doors opposite the ATVs. "Let's try over there."

They drifted off as the group walked down into the mining area. Mark tried the first of the metal doors but found it locked. The next door opened into a locker-type area but with no sign of a toilet. Door number three was more productive, exposing a foyer with a bathroom. Mark waited outside for her, taking a few photos of the work vehicles and carts. When Vanessa emerged, he offered a suggestion.

"How about posing by the lockers for a photo?"

"All right, but we need to catch up to the tour."

"No problem. Here. Let me open the door."

She stood in the doorway, smiling, with the locker room as a backdrop. Mark loved photographing her and felt a little naughty, like they were playing hooky.

"Great shots! All right. Let's get back to school now." Vanessa laughed and held his arm as they set off to rejoin the tour. He wanted to kiss her again, but she was being a chaperone right now. Professionalism overruled.

Outside the mine, Mark set up a group shot of the kids and teachers in front of the Dixie Prospecting sign. The sun of the warm September afternoon gave perfect lighting for the picture. He knew when he pressed the shutter it would be the lead photo for the newspaper story.

As the bus was loading for departure, Vanessa questioned Mark. "When can we look over the pictures?"

"I'll certainly use some with the story." He saw another opportunity. "If you're up for the football game Friday, we can study them in detail afterward."

"All right. It's a date, then." She smiled pleasantly at him.

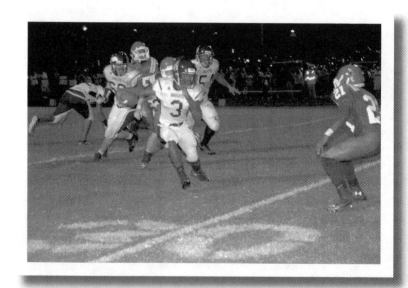

Photo courtesy of *The News Progress*

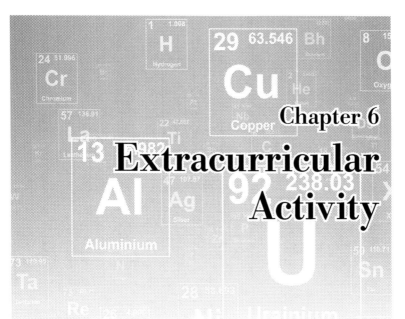

Chapter 6

Extracurricular Activity

Vanessa Foster met Mark at the Friday night football game. Mark stood in his usual game-time position along the Bluestone High School sidelines. His uniform of camera and clipboard established his team role. She noted that he was tall enough that his view was unobstructed by players in full garb and slender enough to not be obtrusive to the sideline action. Vanessa felt an intensified thrill of the game when standing beside him.

"Now, our team's in the blue, right?" she asked.

"Yes, but you know that the press must remain objective in its coverage," Mark said with a serious muse.

"Yeah. Sure, coach." She patted him on the butt and yelled out, "Go Bluestone!"

She was going to make it an interesting night for Mark.

Bluestone was a small school in a rural county, fostering a shallow player base. The school was not usually very competitive in their division. Nevertheless, matched against Randolph Henry, a similar-sized school, they were able to squeeze out an18-12 victory. The home team crowd roared with cheers and whistling, riotously overjoyed. Mark briefly detained the coach as the jubilant players flooded the field house locker room.

"Coach Crawford," he cried, "can you comment on the game strategy you used tonight?"

Mike Crawford beamed as he answered. "Well, Randolph Henry played a good, clean game. We just kept to our power I offense and our boys played well. We're happy for this win tonight!" He smiled at Mark, gave Vanessa an approving nod, and turned toward the gleeful locker room.

The mid-September evening slightly chilled the air as Vanessa and Mark walked close together through the parking lot. She was glad she chose jeans and a sweater instead of a skirt for the event. The excitement of the game lingered as she stood beside her car with Mark.

"I can meet you at the office," said Mark. She gave him a quizzical look. "To view the photos," he added. That had been the furthest thing from her mind.

"Oh, yeah! Sure!" She gave him a quick kiss and opened her car door.

"Okay," said Mark.

She maintained a flirtatious cell phone communication with him throughout the ten-minute commute. At *The News Progress* parking lot, Mark came over and opened her car door.

"I forgot. My laptop is at my apartment," he confessed.

"Okay," she replied. "Let's go there."

"Why don't you just ride with me? Your car will be all right here."

"Okay." She grabbed her purse and opened his passenger door. Mark moved his clipboard and camera from the front seat of his Beretta. He tossed them among the nest of newspapers and scrap notes in the rear.

"I see that this is your mobile office," Vanessa noted. It was certainly not a chick mobile.

Riding home with Mark advanced this from a friendly meeting to a possibly more romantic encounter. Mark's apartment was off Route 47 between Chase City and South Hill. His den was furnished with a navy couch, recliner chair, and a flat screen TV. The style was conservative and certainly not haughty.

"Make yourself at home. I'll get my laptop from the bedroom," said Mark. He smiled and walked out of the den. Vanessa gave pursuit and found herself facing him when he turned around beside the bed. She was eager to raise their relationship to a higher level of intimacy. She wrapped her arms around him and their lips met. The kiss lingered and Mark's warm hands slid up under the back of her sweater, exploring the smooth flesh of her back. Vanessa pulled her sweater off over her head and unbuckled his belt as she pushed him down onto the bed. She unzipped his jeans as he squirmed out of his shirt. He fumbled in the drawer of the bedside table and was successful in finding a condom.

Vanessa tugged Mark's jeans and undershorts down. She discovered that his tall and slender physique was a feature shared by his genitalia. Mark donned his latex sheath as she shed her black jeans and nylon panties. She climbed on top of Mark, feeling the heat from his torso. As her breasts fell against his chest, she felt her breathing quicken. He grabbed her buttocks and pulled her against his lower abdomen. After a few squeezes, he shifted and entered her. She gasped briefly, feeling the warm firmness fill her. Their union quickly climbed to a peak and they melted warmly together.

"I guess we'll check those photos later," said Mark softly.

"Maybe in the morning," she responded, smiling.

D r. Hardy drove to the South Hill ER to answer a late-night ME call. A suspicious death was being investigated. Patty, the charge nurse, had the medical record and the details.

"Apparently, the boyfriend pulled up out front and called for help. He claims she got out of the car to take a leak and accidentally peed on a live electrical wire. He gave us her name and then went to park the car, but he just drove off! Seems he dumped her here and ran."

"Sounds suspicious," said Dr. Hardy.

"Yeah. She was a full code, no pulse or breathing. Unresponsive to resuscitation. She was pronounced at 2314 hours."

"What happened to the boyfriend?" asked Hardy.

"We don't know. The police are looking for him."

Detective Duffer walked up to them as she spoke.

"We got a make on the vehicle but no plates," he said. "With the suspect's description, it's a good chance we'll find him."

"Good," said Dr. Hardy.

The decedent was still in trauma bay one, having not yet been moved to the morgue. She was an adult white female lying face-up on the stretcher. She appeared to be in her mid-thirties, about 160 pounds, with light brown hair. A tracheal tube protruded from her mouth, and Dr. Hardy's exam showed no bruising or cuts to the head and no broken bones. Her gray sweatshirt and pants had been shredded by the ER team and laid in disarray about her. Given her history, Dr. Hardy looked closely at her feet for signs of electrical shock. The left foot had a blackened, puncture-like mark on the side, which was consistent with a contact shock site. The right palm had a larger mark with black discolored edges.

"Did you get a body temp?" he asked.

"96.3," answered Nurse Patty.

"Good. I don't see any traumatic injuries," concluded Dr. Hardy. "But the hand and foot marks are consistent with electrical shocks. Not likely from peeing on a wire, though. Who would do that anyway?"

"Yeah. That's what I thought," said Detective Duffer. "It is probably still an accidental death, but the circumstances are suspicious for a crime. Her companion abandoned her. I'll bet he has something to hide."

"Me too," Hardy responded. "We need to send this one to Richmond for a post." He turned to Patty. "We'll need all her clothing, those sweats, any shoes, and any blood samples you may have drawn."

"No problem," answered Patty.

For Dr. Hardy, jogging was more than just exercise. He found it reduced his stress and gave him a chance to enjoy the outdoors. The autumn afternoon was most inviting for his three-mile run. The sun was low in the sky, its light richer, intensifying the red colors of the sumac leaves along the roadside. He carried a plastic bag to gather the aluminum cans that littered the ditches. Following a weekend, he sometimes collected twenty-five to thirty cans on a run. Once he accumulated a few lawn-size bags of cans, he would take them to the recycling truck in Chase City. He thought about the reported copper thefts along with his aluminum recycling and realized that the mining of industrial metals had become different in the twenty-first century. The chipping away of boulders in a cave had been replaced by picking through scraps and roadside trash. Veins of metal ore were now the ditches and dumpsters. *Hi ho, hi ho.*

The following week, his Wednesday afternoon run was postponed by another ME call. He stood on the peninsula known as the overlook, across the lake from Clarksville. Hardy squinted against the glare of the afternoon sun, mirrored by the water's surface, as he looked out over the bridge construction site. A small congregation of construction workers, police, and rescue personnel populated the scene. Detective Bruce Duffer stood by the body that had prompted this call. The deceased man was draped with a sheet and lay on an orange plastic backboard.

"His name's Wade Panther," said Detective Duffer. "He fell about thirty-five feet off that pylon." Duffer pointed to the third column out. "Landed on the barge. EMS met them at the overlook."

"We dispatched Life Flight helicopter," stated the EMT. "He had skull fractures and was flatlined. Asystole. We called it and canceled Life Flight."

Dr. Hardy pulled back the sheet to examine the body. Mr. Panther had short, salt-and-pepper hair and appeared to be middle-aged. Hardy estimated him to be five ten, 170 pounds. There were dark burgundy blood trails from the left ear and nostril. Dr. Hardy palpated the head and felt mobile bone edges beneath the skin along the left side. This head injury was a lethal wound.

"Was he wearing a hard hat?" Dr. Hardy inquired.

"Yes," answered Duffer. "But it was knocked off on impact. He had just unhooked his safety line, supposedly to adjust his harness after going to the toilet. We think the surface was wet and he just slipped off."

Dr. Hardy continued his physical exam, pressing over the bones. He discovered left-sided rib fractures and instability of the pelvic ring.

"He has findings of sudden deceleration injuries," said Hardy, "typical of falling from a height. The cause of death could have been the head injury or even an aortic rupture."

"So, does he need an autopsy?" asked Duffer.

"I'll call it into Richmond, but I would think so. OSHA will investigate this and will want every detail. I view this as an accidental death."

"Okay," replied Duffer. "Oh, Dr. Hardy, do you remember that lady from the ER that was electrocuted?"

"Yeah. Sure."

"Well, we did find her companion. The car trunk was full of electrical wires and pipes. It seems they were stealing metal from job sites to sell to recyclers. She grabbed a wire that was live. Still an accidental death but during the commission of a crime."

"Wow! I've heard about folks stripping construction sites. I guess it's illegal *and* dangerous."

"Yeah. He's been charged. I suppose she was *charged,* too, so to speak."

"Right!" Dr. Hardy laughed. *A mining accident?* he thought.

Chapter 7

Back to School

*B*lam! The booming retort of the .38-caliber revolver was muffled by Dr. Hardy's ear protectors. He watched as the training associate fired from twelve to twenty-four inches away into a white T-shirt, demonstrating a close-range gunshot powder pattern. Hardy was attending the fall medical examiners training session in Roanoke, Virginia. The PSS Range and Training Center hosted the field demo as the attendees were shown how clothing was processed to bring out powder residue patterns.

In the lecture room, eight T-shirts, stretched over cardboard forms, were laid out over the tables. Each sported a bullet hole from either the handgun or a .30-06 rifle from four different distances. The torn entrances in the fabrics varied in size and shape. A chemical spray was applied that formed a golden orange dye when in the presence of nitrite ions from gunpowder. The reaction was temporary, but a second spraying with a fixative transformed the color to a more permanent bright pink. The white shirts took on a starburst tie-dye appearance with black, yellow, and pink hues.

"There are wide variations in patterns left by weapons, even of the same make," reported the instructor. "So when we evaluate a case, it is imperative to use the suspected weapon itself. We fire it at different distances and compare the patterns to those seen on the victim. This gives us an estimate of the range of the shot."

The next morning, the classroom sessions were held at the Hotel Roanoke. The Virginia Institute of Forensic Medicine, a creation of murder mystery author Patricia Cornwell, sponsored the program. Local medical examiners were an outreach of the four regional ME offices, providing scene visits in remote areas of the state. Such educational events kept them current on state procedures and capabilities.

State police officer Talbot followed the talk on crime scene photography. His lecture was on fingerprinting and DNA, explaining the national DNA data bank. This catalog was named "CODIS" for Combined DNA Index System.

"Criminals have gotten wiser. They learn from TV shows and fellow inmates. Gloves and bleach usage have become common. The bleach denatures blood proteins and surface DNA, essentially cleaning the scene of evidence." Dr. Hardy felt their ME work was becoming more futile, the bad guys more calculating.

"There is a new procedure on the horizon," Talbot announced. "It's not in use yet, but research is showing promising results. It's called 'vapors analysis.' An air sample from a crime scene is collected and trace odors are extracted. Body odors, sweat evaporation, perfumes, deodorants, gunpowder smells can be isolated for comparison with suspects. Water vapor in expired air contains some particles that may eventually yield DNA samples.

"It will have significant limitations, of course. It will be most useful in closed rooms and at scenes that are fresh."

Dr. Hardy felt this was verging on science fiction, maybe a glimpse of the future in crime investigations. He would withhold judgment until its utility was shown fruitful.

The final talk was given by a member of the Virginia Funeral Directors Association on the disposition of bodies. There were four basic dispositions: A—Anatomical donation, B—Burial, C—Cremation, or D—Deportation (transporting to another state or country). The traditional methods had evolved little over time, but A variation in cremation had arisen. Chemical cremation, the process of alkaline hydrolysis, had become commonplace in Europe, and several units had been sold in Virginia. Usage in the United States had not yet been given legislative approval, as the disposal of the liquid waste created required regulation as biowaste. The simple basics were potassium hydroxide and lye being mixed with water to dissolve body tissues. Heating the mixture under pressure accelerated the process. All that remained afterward were bones, no identifiable tissue or DNA. Hence, a ME certificate would need to be signed prior to an alkaline hydrolysis, just as in a traditional cremation, to assure evidence was not destroyed.

"As with burned cremations," the funeral director said, "there are still bony cremains to crush or bury."

Dr. Hardy suddenly recalled the skeletonized body he had reported on from the lake beach. The bones had been so clean—he had assumed from sand and sunlight. If the body had undergone alkaline hydrolysis, the remains might have been the result of a more recent death. This would mean the investigation might need to broaden its scope.

Promptly following Dr. Hardy's medical education conference, he and Lucy returned to work at the medical practice. When they finished the day's business duties, they anxiously drove out to their home construction site to meet with Greg Jackson. The flooring boards had been stacked inside to acclimate before installing, but the geothermal heat pumps had broken down. They were fed by underground water from the well.

"There's only nine gallons per minute flowing from the well," Greg reported. "The geothermals need twenty gallons per minute."

"But our well driller measured over thirty gallons per minute," said Hardy. "That's why we chose the open system!"

"That's true," said Hatcher, the well driller. He was on location with Greg. "We checked it again and it was right. But we let it run for three to four hours, and then the flow dropped. It seems there is a large pocket, or reservoir, of water underground. After it is drained, the aquifer runs at nine gallons per minute."

"Crap!" Hardy exclaimed. "The closed systems cost so much more!" He chose the geothermal units as they were priced only ten percent above conventional heat pumps and were much more energy efficient. The open systems pulled water from an underground source and then dumped it in a drain ditch. Closed units were more like a car radiator that recirculated the fluid but required a lengthy underground pipe system. "I wonder if it would work if we dug a second well."

"I don't know," Hatcher stated. "You might still not get enough flow. It's a hit or miss."

"It would be the quickest solution," said Greg.

Quickness is not a trait you've displayed so far, thought Hardy. "Okay. We'll try that."

"All right. But we can't put the flooring down until we have a stable temperature inside," continued Greg.

"Well, the upstairs unit only pulls eight gallons per minute. You can still run that one," said Hardy as a suggestion.

"Okay," Greg said in agreement. He pulled two cold beers from his cooler and offered one to Hatcher. Hatcher shook his head and declined. Greg popped open his can and gulped.

"It's not really a time to celebrate," Dr. Hardy whispered to Lucy. Then, turning to Greg, he asked, "How long do you think this will take us to do?"

Greg looked at Hardy and smiled. "Looks like about another 4 to 6 weeks till we're done."

M ark McClain didn't travel to all of Bluestone's away games, but this Friday was a priority. They were playing Prince Edward in Farmville, the town where Vanessa lived. From there, she had a short commute to the SVCC campus. Farmville was a college town, home to Longwood University and nearby Hampden-Sydney College. It had a trendy and upbeat flair, attractive to yuppies. Unfortunately, high school athletics were upstaged by collegiate programs and often went unnoticed. Mark's press pass only worked for home games, so he had to shuck up the five-dollar admission. He took his position along the visitor's sidelines. That's where Vanessa found him.

"You know we're pulling for opposing teams tonight," she said in jest.

"Well, you know that the press must remain objective."

"Bullshit!" she injected, and bumped him with her hip. "Let's go,

Prince Edward!" she yelled from the Bluestone sideline. Mark smiled and shook his head. He had his work cut out for him keeping up with her.

Vanessa's cheering seemed to help the home team, as the PE Eagles handed Bluestone a twenty-eight to six loss.

"All right, you loser!" she said, smiling cheerfully. "You need to buy me a drink at Applebee's so I can celebrate winning." That sounded more like a win for Mark.

"Okay," he agreed.

Mark was putting away his second draft beer as Vanessa sat beside him at the bar, sipping her daiquiri. Her hair was dark brown, nearly black, and full of body. She wore a burgundy sweater and he envisioned her bronzed torso flowing beneath the knit fabric as she moved.

"What are you thinking?" she asked.

"Oh, nothing. Just relaxing." He leaned in and kissed her. "I guess I've got a drive home."

"Don't rush it! Can you come by my place first?" she pleaded.

You won't have to ask twice, he thought. "Okay, sure."

He followed Vanessa to her apartment on the south end of town. *It's even on the way home*, he thought. Her place was a comfortable appearing two-bedroom apartment. She had one bedroom set up as an office, and she took his hand and led him into the other one. She lit a candle in front of the mirror on her dresser and sat beside him on the bed.

Her lips were moist and warm as they kissed, and Mark felt a little giddy from the beer and his rising passion. He reached under her sweater which, as if on cue, she pulled off over her head. His arousal intensified as she helped him remove his pants. She kneeled down to pull his feet through the pant legs, giving him an enticing view of her cleavage. Her bra was black and low cut, her breasts bulging up in the center. She stayed on the floor and gently stroked him before guiding him to her lips. The warm, soft touch of her mouth was ecstatic as he felt his heartbeat pulsing in his head, the rate quickening. As he felt the first waves of orgasm approaching, she released him from her mouth, still fondling him with her hands. At his peak, she firmly pinched down on the end of his organ, holding back his fluid for two pulsations. She then quickly released him and the built up pressure caused him to spurt a strong stream about two feet out.

"Ahhh," he moaned in rapture. He had never felt a surge so powerful. His body seemed to melt.

"Paper boy," she cooed, appearing pleased with her work. "I call that a 'press release,'"

"Definitely!" he responded with staccato breathing.

She pulled off her jeans and bra and slid the covers over Mark and herself.

"I think I'm ready for a special edition," she teased. Mark smiled and pulled her warm body against his. This sensual bliss was more intoxicating than the beer. He was in no rush to leave here.

The soft beep from Mark's phone signaled a text message. He ignored it, afraid it might be Yvonne. This was heaven and he'd have no intrusion from worldly matters. He focused his attention on cuddling Vanessa, but his phone toned again. He sighed and turned to identify the cellular intruder.

"It's Dad!" he said aloud.

"What?" she asked.

"He's stranded. I'm sorry, but I've got to go!" Mark reached for his clothes. "He drives for the rescue squad and the ambulance has broken down."

"Oh. Sure, of course. Can I help you?"

"I don't know." He didn't want to exclude her, but this would probably not interest her.

"Can I come with you? I could keep you company." She had already put on her bra and was pulling up her jeans.

"Sure, if you want to." He tried to hide his delight.

While en route, he called his dad back and learned he was at the Quik Stop in Chase City. They arrived at about one forty-five after a thirty-minute commute. A box-shaped ambulance with burgundy trim stripes was parked near the fuel pump and confirmed the location. Mr. McClain stood in the store holding his second cup of coffee. Mark introduced Vanessa to his father, Buddy McClain, who nodded approvingly.

"Sorry, son. This is old Unit 11, a 1995 model. It began cutting off on us back in the summer. Usually, if we waited ten or fifteen minutes, it would crank," Mr. McClain explained. "Tonight it just died!"

"Did you call a mechanic?" asked Mark.

"Yeah. Charles Homes. He can haul it in in the morning." Homes' Garage had a contract with Mecklenburg County to maintain the sheriff's office vehicles. If the county trusted their police cruisers with that shop, it seemed natural that Boydton Life Station would take their ambulances there as well.

"All right, Dad. Let's get you home."

After Mark delivered Buddy McClain to Boydton and returned to Chase City, it was two thirty in the morning.

"I guess I'll get you back home now," said Mark.

"It's pretty late," said Vanessa, yawning.

"You want to just crash at my place, then?" offered Mark.

"Yeah. That sounds better."

Once under the covers, Vanessa pressed her bare breasts against Mark's chest.

"Now, where were we?" she said softly. Mark smiled. There was no way he had forgotten.

He slept soundly after the long night and feeling the comfort of Vanessa's warm, soft skin.

A tapping at his door startled him awake. He hadn't heard the text tone and just now read the missed message. It was from Yvonne at seven thirty: *Just got off. On the way over to sleep. You still in bed?* She had a key to his place! Mark sprang out of bed and into his den as his door opened. Smiling, Yvonne stepped in, dressed in fuchsia scrubs, her hair in dreadlocks.

"Who is it, Mark?" called Vanessa from the bedroom. Yvonne's smile was gone, her eyes glaring at Mark.

"It's nothing," answered Mark.

"Nothing?" said Yvonne, then vehemently repeated, *"Nothing?"*

"Look, Yvonne. I was going to tell you, but—"

Yvonne threw his apartment key across the room. "Just forget it!" She stormed out the door, slamming it closed as she left. Vanessa came in, wearing Mark's shirt, just in time to hear the squeal of car tires.

"A friend of yours?" she asked.

"Yeah," said Mark, turning toward her. "She used to be." He smiled weakly. The past twenty-four hours had been a roller coaster ride, but he wasn't ready to get off. He felt so alive.

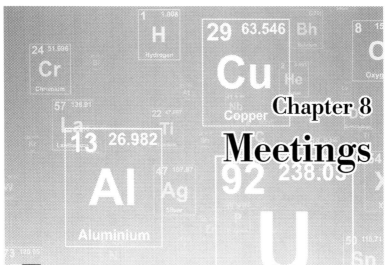

Chapter 8

Meetings

James Callahan had placed a large map on his bulletin board displaying the three counties sponsoring the governor's school students. The counties were subdivided into areas according to zip code assignments. He had collated all of the radon testing results of his Science 101 students on a summary sheet.

"You each now have the cumulative report of the individual radon readings with your initials and the corresponding zip code of each test site. There are colored pins by the bulletin board that represent result ranges. The readings are expressed in picocuries per liter, or pCi/L. The white pin is less than 1 pCi/L, pink pins are 1 to 2 pCi/L, yellows are 2 to 3, oranges are 3 to 4, and red is over 4. First thing today, each of you will place the appropriate colored pin on the map at your test site. They are sectioned off by zip code zones to help you. Okay, go up and tag your spots."

When the scuffle and chatter of excited teenagers waned, Callahan continued. "You can see the report is separated by counties. Who can tell us the hypothesis for this study?" Andy Francis's hand promptly shot up. "Okay, Andy."

"Are there regional differences in radon levels in Virginia counties?" Andy answered eagerly.

"That's right! Now, to prove this, we need to average the readings for each county and apply the chi-square test analysis to obtain a p value probability score."

Vikki Hardy whispered to Andy at the table beside hers. "You're such a geek!" She gave him a smirk of a smile.

"Shh!" he responded.

At the end of class, the map was speckled with white, pink, and a few yellow pins. Of the twenty-eight markers, there were no reds and only two orange pins, both in Harrison County. Callahan noted to himself this curiosity but decided to withhold drawing any conclusions before the statistics were compiled.

After dismissing class, Callahan retreated to the staff lounge. Vanessa was seated on the couch studying her laptop. He had always found her attractive and today was no exception. He smiled at her as he opened the refrigerator.

"What's so interesting, Vanessa?" he asked.

"Just some busy work," she replied. "Oh, you never saw all of the tungsten mine photos, did you?"

"Naw. Just those you showed me in the newspaper," he said, opening a can of Sundrop.

"Okay. I'll pull them up for you." He sat down beside her on the couch as she clicked open the file. She moved slowly through the gallery of images.

"All right. These are great!" Callahan admired the photos but suddenly stopped her. "Hey, what's that? Back up one." She had rushed through the shot of her outside the toilet.

"Oh. I had just wandered off to find the bathroom," she explained.

"What was that?"

"Just some locker area." Callahan leaned closer. Something seemed a bit odd to him.

"Can you zoom in on those lockers there?" he pointed.

"Sure. Okay." The photo grew larger. Callahan focused on the yellow protective suits hanging behind Vanessa. They had hoods and respirator masks. These suits were not standard mining wear.

"Those are radiation protective suits!" he exclaimed.

"What? Those suits?"

"Yes! I'm certain."

"But, why would they need those?" asked Vanessa.

"They wouldn't," Callahan concluded. He realized that radon

seepage could present exposure hazards in underground mining, but it would be monitored and minimized by an adequate ventilation system. "What are radiation suits doing at that tungsten mine?" he pondered aloud. He turned to Vanessa and found her looking at him with a worried expression.

"Runners, take your mark … Go!" Lucy Hardy called out. She stood beside Business Route 58, in front of the medical office. Twelve runners took stride on her command, starting the annual five-mile run. It was Boydton Day, and this run had been sponsored by Dr. Hardy's office for twenty years. He, himself, was a participant, winking at Lucy as he trod off. The course traversed the town's main drag, today bordered on each side by booths and tables of local vendors. The smoke from the waning stewpot fires spiced the air, already flavored by the aroma of Brunswick stew. At forty-eight degrees, the October morning was a little brisk, but the sky was clear and the rich light of the early sun enhanced the autumn foliage.

"Pick 'em up, Doc!" hollered Alan Hancock from the rescue squad concession booth as the runners passed by.

"All right!" answered Dr. Hardy. "You need to join us next year!"

"Sure thing." Alan smiled.

Dr. Hardy finished in second place, outshined by the well-trained marathon veteran who had won three years in a row. After the race was complete, Lucy and Obie Hardy wandered the streets, browsing the marketplace. Vikki and Anna were readying to march in the parade with the school band.

Boydton Day was always a week or two before elections, making it a politician's field day. State Senator Sidney Francis was present, shaking hands and smiling along the parade route. The county rivaled high school bands were separated by floats. The Association to Preserve Mecklenburg had sponsored a float with pine trees, a cow, a deer, and a man fishing. "No Ethanol Plant" signs were mounted along the base.

Walking through the crowded street after the parade, Dr. Hardy met Detective Duffer.

"Bruce," he greeted. "I was hoping I'd see you."

"Oh yeah? What's up?" he asked.

"Any progress on ID'ing the bones from Buffalo Junction?"

"Nope. No leads yet. Why?"

"I just attended an ME conference and heard about chemical cremations, or so-called alkaline hydrolysis. Apparently, using an alkali like lye can reduce a body to just bones in days to weeks."

"Yeah. I've heard about that too."

"Well, those bones were so clean of body tissues and debris, I had figured it had taken at least six months of exposure to the elements. But, if someone processed a body in lye, it may have taken only days after the death."

"Hmm," said Duffer pensively. "That means we could expand our time window on possible missing persons. That might help."

"It was just a thought," said Hardy. "Oh. The alkaline hydrolysis destroys most DNA evidence as well."

"Yeah. This means it's likely that a murder was involved," Duffer added.

"Yeah. I guess so." Their discussion ended abruptly as Vikki and Anna walked up. They wore jackets but were still dressed in their band pants and shoes. They were smiling, having completed their marching performance.

"Are you guys hungry?" asked Lucy.

"No," said Anna.

"They fed us Subway at the fire station," Vikki explained.

"But we need some money for the competition," Anna added. The buses were leaving from there for the Greenville County band competition. Boydton Day for the Hardy girls was nearly over now.

"Okay," said Dr. Hardy. He handed them each ten dollars for supper.

"Call us on the way home," said Lucy.

"Sure," said Vikki.

"Thanks!" Anna added as they bounded off down the street.

The original Boydton Life Station's double-wide headquarters had been removed to accommodate their new building construction. Their pro tempore home base was an old vacant, fuel-oil trucking yard. The cinderblock-walled office was ten by sixteen feet, adjoining an aluminum garage. About fifteen members crowded into the garage area for their monthly business meeting. Alan Hancock addressed the assembly.

"Our new building is coming along," Alan began. "The cement has been poured, the steel framing set, and the roof is on. We did have some vandalism last month, some stolen pipes and wire. After our second monthly loan draw, we're close to schedule.

"Now, as you all know, Unit 11 has spent more time in the shop than on the road over the past six months. Largely due to what Homes calls a 'vapor lock,' something the new fuel-injected engines avoid. It's a 1995 model with 162,000 miles on it. It's served us well, but we need to replace it. We can buy a new Ford Econoline for $98,000. Selling the old one might bring us 6 to 12 thousand."

"Do we have that kind of money?" asked Buddy McClain.

"Well, no. Della, what's our balance?"

"Current checking balance is $32,682," the treasurer reported. "That's including the $1,652 we raised on Boydton Day barbecue sales."

"We put in a request for an ODEMSA state funding grant," said Hancock. "We may hear from that this month. They sometimes respond with a fifty-fifty matching grant where we would still need to raise our 50 percent."

"We could have a raffle to raise money," someone said.

"Yeah. Maybe get some electronics donated to raffle," another member added.

"All right," Hancock said. "With the sale of our old ambulance and some fund raisers, I think we could make the fifty-fifty matching funding amount."

"I move that we set a goal to raise $10,000 over the next six months for a new ambulance," McClain proposed.

"I second it," said Treasurer Della. The motion carried unanimously.

Walter Snelling of Dixie Prospecting telephoned Vanessa for his monthly update.

"So you've joined the Association to Preserve Mecklenburg, huh?" he asked.

"Right. It's a small group of citizens, not heavily funded. They only have donations to work with," Vanessa explained. "They did sponsor a float in the Boydton Day parade."

"Any word on uranium mining?"

"Not really. It's been mentioned at meetings, but we're largely focused on the ethanol plant. The group narrow-mindedly opposes the plant. Although I feel the community would greatly benefit from it." Vanessa didn't air these views at meetings unless someone asked her directly. Her role was primarily to obtain information useful to Snelling, her contractor, but she wasn't about to compromise her values.

"All right. I'm sending you $500 to donate to the group. Give it in your name. Try to keep them focused on the ethanol plant controversy."

"Okay. Sure."

"Thanks. We'll talk again next month."

"Fine. I'll talk to you then."

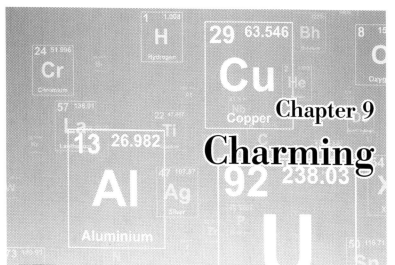

Chapter 9

Charming

The county's weekly crime report listed arrests, traffic violations, and convictions. *The News Progress* would not print these items unless the court service gave them a certified notice or faxed the information directly from its office. The editor preferred to have original documents, usually picked up by a staff reporter. Mark McClain was retrieving the report this week. He read over the list the clerk's assistant had handed to him.

"Oh. The bones were identified!" he exclaimed. Then, looking back to the assistant, he asked, "Is anyone available who can give me details on this case?"

"I'll see," she said, and then walked away from her desk. She returned promptly and announced, "Detective Bruce Duffer can talk with you now. Just go over to the sheriff's office and ask for him."

"Thanks!"

Detective Duffer met Mark and led him back to a small conference room.

"So tell me about identifying the bones," said Mark.

"Well, initially, we had no leads," Detective Duffer explained. "The remains were skeletal, believed to be six to twelve months old. There were no identifying clues, no clothing or jewelry, and no corresponding missing persons. On a hunch, we broadened our window for missing persons and ID'd a fifty-two-year-old male, Phil Bentley."

"Do you know his cause of death?" the reporter probed.

"No. It's still undetermined."

"When was Mr. Bentley last seen?" Mark knew this story was newsworthy.

"April 19. He was in Louisa County to inspect the vermiculite quarry. He worked for the state: the DMME—Division of Mines, Minerals, and Energy."

"Do you know how he ended up here, in Mecklenburg County?"

"Not yet. It's still under investigation." Duffer sounded a little disappointed. Back when Mark pulled rescue squad duty, he frequently responded to fire department calls. Duffer was a volunteer firefighter and often worked alongside Mark when he fought fires. This camaraderie with the detective sometimes enabled Mark to extract details that were not meant to be released without seeming intrusive or offensive.

"Bruce," Mark said, and then lowered his voice. "Is there anything else you can tell me? Maybe off the record?" He pocketed his pen and smiled innocently.

Duffer looked at Mark for a moment, contemplating his response. "Well, *totally* off the record, and you can't breathe a word of this!" Mark nodded sincerely. "When they did the autopsy, they found traces of radioactivity."

"What? Where would that come from?"

"We have no idea. And that *can't* be released! Can you imagine the panic it could cause?"

"Oh, yeah," Mark agreed. "Absolutely!"

The slowly growing Clarksville Bridge columns now spanned the lake's breadth like stepping-stones to the town. They appeared as black towers against the orange glow of the dusk sky. Dr. Hardy drove across the old bridge en route to his weekly rounds at Meadowview Terrace Nursing Home. He had attended patients there since its opening in 2001. The nursing units were called neighborhoods and named after flowers, reflecting the "meadow" of its name.

Dr. Hardy was to see a lady named Carolyn Schmidt on Water Lilly Lane, who had been there two months following a stroke. At eighty-two, she was still lucid and lively, despite her balance and vision problems from the stroke.

"Ms. Schmidt," he asked, "has your balance improved any from the physical therapy?"

"Call me Carolyn," she responded. "My last name sounds too much like 'shit'! And there's enough of that around here!"

"Okay, Carolyn."

"Well, I have improved. But, if I try to walk without the walker, I fall into the wall. I can't half see either."

"The progress after a stroke is slow. Don't be impatient."

"Oh. I have written some poems. They printed one in the monthly newsletter here."

"Very good! I'll get one and read it."

"Take this one," she said. She pulled it out of her bedside table drawer. "I've got a dozen of them!"

"Thanks." He told himself he would read it tonight.

"You know, I've figured out what this place reminds me of. It's God's waiting room. These people are lying around, decrepit, worn out—just waiting. Then God looks down and calls, 'Next.'"

A sobering image, thought Hardy.

His next patient was Garland Geer, a sixty-two-year-old white man afflicted with cerebral palsy since birth. He had never walked and spent all of his life in nursing homes, moving to Meadowview shortly after it opened. He had an anatomic variant where his colon looped up against his diaphragm. This caused him to develop chest pains and shortness of breath whenever he became constipated.

"Hey, Garland," greeted Hardy. "How've you been?"

"Hey, Dr. Hardy. Pretty good, I guess." He was a pleasant man with spastic motions of his upper limbs and grimacing facial movements when he spoke.

"Any trouble with your bowel movements recently?"

"No," he answered. Then he raised his cheeks in a squinting type movement and said, softly, "Not since that night nurse put a spell on me."

"A spell? From a nurse here?" Hardy inquired.

"Yeah, Julie. She's a witch, they say." He smiled at Dr. Hardy.

"All right. Well, I'm glad it's working." Dr. Hardy found the story incredulous but welcomed the favorable outcome. In medicine, the placebo effect is when someone experiences a positive therapeutic effect by suggestion only—believing that something works. Placebo response rates are reported as high as fifteen to twenty percent. Homeopathic, placebo, or witchcraft effect, Hardy only cared that Garland was doing well. He shook his head as he walked back to the charting area.

The first week of December heralded an annual routine for the Hardy family: visiting their timeshare week at Massenutten Mountain Resort. Dr. Hardy had purchased week forty-nine in 1980, early in the resort's development. They picked up their daughters from school early on Thursday to leave for their long weekend escape. Lucy drove their van through Chase City on the way out of the county. Many of the roadside driveways around the town displayed the yellow No Ethanol Plant signs.

"What's so bad about an ethanol plant here?" Lucy asked.

"I don't know," answered Obie Hardy. "We certainly need some local industry."

"I've heard it's about the odor from the fermented mash," Lucy said. "You know what it's like around paper mill plants."

"I reckon so." Dr. Hardy thumbed through the week's *News Progress* paper. "Hey, you remember those bones we found in Buffalo Junction?"

"Yeah," answered Lucy. "Why?"

"They've identified them as a missing person, Phil Bentley. It appears he was an inspector for Virginia DMME—Division of Mines, Minerals, and Energy. He was last seen in Louisa."

"Do they know what happened?" Lucy asked.

"No. It says the case is still under investigation."

They travelled north of Farmville on Route 15 as the terrain grew more rolling, having reached the foothills. The first mountain they encountered was Willis Mountain, the site of the world's oldest and largest kyanite mine.

"Wow! They've certainly dug a chunk out of that mountain!" Obie Hardy exclaimed.

"What for?" asked Vikki.

"I guess it's strip mining. This is said to be one of the few kyanite mines in the world."

"Oh! Professor Callahan told us about kyanite!" said Vikki.

"I don't know what it's used for. I've heard airplane metals or something," Obie Hardy said.

"You're close, Dad. It's a silicate mineral, very heat resistant. It was used in the heat-shield tiles of the space shuttle but usually in more everyday things like insulators, porcelain, and car brake shoes."

"Thank you, Miss Geologist," Lucy said.

Completing the three-hour drive, the Hardys settled into a condo in the Summit phase of Massenutten Resort, looking out over the valley and the tiny, shining lights of Elkton. Lucy started heating the frozen pizzas and assembling a salad. Dr. Obie Hardy opened a bottle of rosé wine, poured two glasses, and handed one to Lucy. This was a haven, no hospital rounds or beepers for at least three days. Vikki had the TV on and Anna was sitting in the floor playing cards. Anna was wearing a black Harley-Davidson T-shirt, black jeans, and ankle-high boots. High school is a developmental stage where kids seek out their identities. Lucy called this Anna's "gothic phase" and Daddy Hardy desperately hoped it was just that—a phase. From a toddler, she had been infatuated with cards: playing cards, business cards, credit cards, ID cards—all types. Sipping on his wine, Obie looked in on her game from over her shoulder. He saw her shuffling an unusual deck of colorful, oversized cards. She spread out the cards facedown and touched them gently as if they were a live pet.

"What kind of cards are they, Anna?"

"Tarot cards," she said flatly, without looking up. Her black nail polish flashing as she handled the cards.

"Tarot cards? Do they tell fortunes?" Obie inquired.

"Shhh! I'm doing a reading!" Anna snapped. Apparently, he had disturbed her karma or spiritual zone. He softly stepped back but continued to study her actions. She pulled out a card and turned it face-up, revealing a drawing with four golden cups. After pausing, as if completely absorbing the image, she dealt a second card alongside it. It was a type of face card. She touched each of them slowly before drawing the third card. This one displayed what looked like the castle in chess game pieces. "Hmm," she sighed.

"What do the cards say?" Obie asked.

"Shh!" she snapped, as if the aura was disrupted. After sitting a few moments in a weighted silence, she shook her head slowly. Obie took a sip of his wine. "It's not like a simple statement," she stated. "It's a feeling, a sense, a summation of life's factors."

"Oh." Obie responded, now completely captivated. "So, what are they *sensing*?"

"The first card encompasses the past. The four of cups could symbolize our family of four. The cups are a fullness, a time to count blessings, making sound decisions to proceed with a planned course."

"Like building our new house?" posed Obie.

"Yeah, most likely." She then continued, "The second card is the present. It's upside down, a reverse reading. That means its meaning is more powerful, more intense. The knight of pentacles. That's a warning that it's time to focus on work or projects. It's not a time to take chances or gamble!"

"That's a little unsettling," Obie said. Then, more hopefully, he asked, "So what's the last card? A rook, or a castle?"

"The tower card! The future! It foretells darkness and destruction on a physical scale. It may represent ambitions that are based on false pretenses." She looked up solemnly at her father. Despite the warmth he was feeling from the wine, Obie felt a chill creep through his body. *Could this mean the new house?* he thought.

"Supper's ready," announced Lucy. Anna and Vikki scurried to the table. Obie took a lingering look at the ominous three cards, feeling somewhat moved by their message.

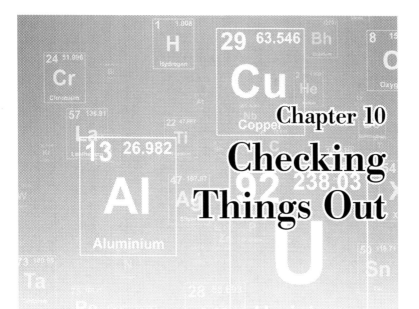

Chapter 10

Checking Things Out

Dr. Hardy's winter retreat was too short-lived as he returned to his office practice routine on Monday. Geraldine Bouldin presented with a gynecological problem. She was a hefty, 210-pound black lady in exam room two.

"I've had this discharge from my ann-gina for three to four weeks," she reported. Dr. Hardy detected a slight musty scent in the exam room, or maybe it was an imaginary fabrication. "Since I'm late for my minister, I was wondering if it's a problem with my odories."

Unless he was mistaken, Dr. Hardy felt that her "odories" were functioning fine. "Okay, we'll need to do a female exam to check this out."

"All right," she responded. Dr. Hardy stepped out while Nurse Lucy and the patient prepared for the pelvic exam. When he reentered the room, Dr. Hardy was certain there was a lingering pungent smell. When he looked at Lucy, she wrinkled up her nose.

"Okay," Dr. Hardy said. "I'm placing the speculum now." He found a grayish discharge present in the vaginal opening and, apparently, an object coated with it, not unlike biscuits and gravy. "I need a sponge forceps and a basin," he directed Lucy. She abandoned the routine swabs and Pap prep she had readied and handed him the instrument and the stainless steel emesis basin. He reached in with the forceps and grasped the spongy mass, noting an attached fiber-like substance. "I think there's a string in here," he commented and pulled the conglomerate out, depositing it into the basin.

"Oh!" exclaimed Geraldine. "That's my tam-poon! I don't remember removing the last one!"

A horrendous smell erupted, engulfing the room with the fetid fumes. Lucy gagged twice and suddenly left the room. Dr. Hardy, with his eyes watering from the potent stench, turned and deposited the rotting glob into the hazardous waste can in the room. Emerging from the exam room, he announced to Loren and Lucy, "Let's close room two for the rest of the day!"

During lunch break, Greg Jackson came by Hardy's office to give a construction update.

"I got the permits for drilling the three wells for the geothermals," he said. Hardy, himself, had drawn up the paperwork and explained to the health department officials that they were not wells for water, since they only would approve one well per homesite. "Hatcher can dig them this week. I'm using the emergency electric heat on the units to acclimate the wooden flooring before laying it."

"Okay," remarked Hardy, feeling glad to hear there was some progress.

"The AC people say the wells need to be filled with betonite when the piping is placed. Supposedly, it's a mud-like substance that will conduct heat well. We can't find out where to get this stuff yet."

"All right. When will we be ready for the carpeting?"

"In about two weeks."

"So the week before Christmas?"

"Yeah."

"Okay. I'll schedule the carpet people for then." Greg's slothful progress had led Hardy to undertake some of the contracting himself, pushing the well permit paperwork and finding the carpet installer. Greg's carpet-layers were reportedly booked up for a couple of months.

"Fine," said Greg. Hardy felt an auspicious glimmer as Jackson left. His mortgage quote would expire on January 1.

On Tuesday, Boydton Life Station held their monthly business meeting at the vacated trucking base again. It was a bitter cold night, forcing the members to huddle into the small, cinderblock office area. Treasurer Della gave the financial report.

"Our current balance is $38,416. We have some great prizes donated for our raffle and, if we sell all our tickets, we could clear $5,000."

"Anybody who has sold their packet of tickets can pick up another pack and turn your money into Della," Hancock announced. "Now, on our building construction, the last monthly bank draw was $35,000. This bill included brick-laying and electrical. Obviously, the brick work is incomplete. The left side of the building is only half-done. The bank inspector has questioned the electrical work, since it doesn't appear completed either."

"What does this mean?" a squad member asked.

"Well, they already paid the draw. But they're going to have another contractor appraise the amount of electrical work completed. I guess they'll hold back from the next draw based on the estimate they get back."

"I hope we don't get swindled," the member added.

"Well, on a positive note, we were awarded the ODEMSA fifty-fifty grant for a new ambulance. We'll need to sell Unit 11 and complete our fund-raising. I suggest we list Unit 11 for sale at 18 to 20 thousand dollars," Hancock said.

"I move that we list Unit 11 for sale at $20,000," said Buddy McClain.

"I second that," another member added.

"All in favor say 'aye,'" Hancock said. It carried unanimously.

Virginia's legislative session was winding down for the year and a cocktail reception afforded a welcomed break. The Commonwealth Club on Franklin Street was an alluring site for such an event. Mark McClain's paper carried a monthly report from Senator Francis. McClain received the senator's synopsis of the evening's events. Sidney Francis was known for keeping lobbyists at a distance but accepted this invitation, probably because of the appeal of the club. Originally, the Commonwealth Club was an aristocratic southern gentlemen's club, but financial pressures had led it to become much more open. Its rich heritage and colonial charm emanated from the tall windows, crown molding, and intricate wood trim.

Three adjoining rooms each had display tables and an open bar with heavy hors d'oeuvres carried by formally attired servers. The first room was for the United Mine Workers of America, the UMWA, representing the coal miners from far western Virginia. Their promotional poster had a map highlighting its US District 17, covering eastern Kentucky, West Virginia, Tennessee, and Virginia. Stars marked the subdistrict office in Castlewood and the international office base near Quantico. The second room drew support from the shipping docks in the eastern coastal cities, largely the Port of Richmond, Norfolk, and the Virginia Port Authority. Their group was a subsidiary of the International Longshoreman's Association, which prospered during the World War I period. The ILA acronym was promoted as synonymous with "I Love America". In the 1950s, their name was tarnished as accusations of gangsterism flourished. Their new and improved philanthropic image was projected by their poster touting the $2,500 in funds they had raised for the 2009 Haitian relief drive. The struggling island of Haiti had been bombarded by four consecutive hurricanes.

Lastly, Dixie Prospecting was the sponsor of the third room. Their poster boasted a diagrammed drawing of a cement-lined storage bunker covered with a layer of gravel, then soil, and a beautifully green bed of grass. DP marketing agent, Neal Hooker, mingled with the lawmakers, all smiles and handshakes. He greeted Sidney Francis in this manner.

"Senator Francis," he said. "You have Harrison County in your district, right?"

"Yes, I do," answered Francis flatly.

"The economic effect a uranium mine would have on your district would be phenomenal! I'm sure you'll carefully consider lifting the1982 mining ban."

Francis accepted a stuffed mushroom from a passing tray and sipped his gin and tonic. "We're still reviewing the safety data. There have been no uranium mines in a temperate climate zone in the world, let alone the United States."

"That's right, sir. Our mining techniques are twenty-first century and pose no potential environmental threats. Coal-burning, electrical-generating plants release more radiation into the environment than uranium mining would. Studies have shown that coal ash has one hundred times more radiation than is released from a nuclear plant producing the same amount of electricity."

"The Virginia Beach study of the effect a hurricane would have on contamination of Buggs Island Lake is scary. I haven't seen enough safety data to support lifting the ban on mining yet."

"I see," replied Mr. Hooker. "Well, please look over our safety display. It does have some impressive science to back it."

"Okay. But the jury is still out on this."

"All right. Well, enjoy the refreshments." Neal Hooker gave a sinister closing smile and moved on to woo the next legislator.

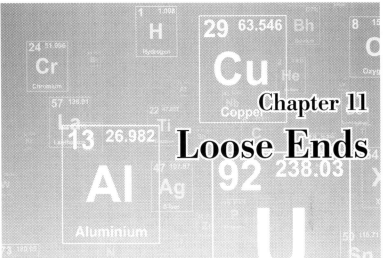

Chapter 11

Loose Ends

Mark McClain's curiosity had simmered, leading him to phone the Virginia DMME office in Charlottesville. He was transferred to Phil Bentley's supervisor.

"Yes, I worked with Phil Bentley," said the supervisor. "I've spoken with a detective already. A Duffer, I believe."

"Sure, Detective Duffer. I was hoping you might do me a favor and clarify a few of the details for the press story. This is all off the record, unless you tell me specifically that I can use an item."

"All right. We all liked Phil and want to find out what happened."

"Detective Duffer said he was last seen in Louisa on April 19, correct?"

"That was the vermiculite quarry. A very routine inspection."

"What was his next assignment?"

"Dixie Prospecting. They had filed for an exploratory drilling permit in Harrison County, looking for uranium. He had a scheduled inspection of their site that afternoon, and then Willis Mountain the next day, April 20. He did check in to a motel near there that night. Sprouses Corner, that's where his car was found."

"So, did he make it to Harrison?" McClain asked.

"Oh, yes. The site manager, Walter Snelling, confirmed his visit there and we received his evaluation report from that site."

"He sent in the paperwork?"

"Yeah. Well, not paperwork, actually. He sent in his report by computer."

"I see." Mark sensed something out of the ordinary had transpired. "So when did he check into the motel?"

"About 2 a.m."

"On April 20, then. Right?"

"Yeah."

"So he never made it to Willis Mountain, then?"

"Nope. I guess they lucked out on that."

"What do you mean?"

"That's a hornet's nest if ever there was! He cited them for three violations a few months back and was returning for a reevaluation. They were at risk of being shut down."

"So they had a lot at stake in this inspection,"

"Absolutely!"

"Thank you for your help. Oh, do you have a photo of Phil Bentley that you could fax to me?"

"I guess so. His DMME ID photo, if that's okay."

"Yeah. Sure. That would be great! Thanks."

Mark was energized by the Phil Bentley story and was always looking for any chance to see Vanessa again.

"Vanessa," he said when she answered his phone call. "How far is Farmville from Sprouses Corner?"

"Oh, about thirty minutes, I guess. Why?"

"Are you up for a road trip this weekend?"

"Sure. To Sprouses Corner?" The town was little more than a crossroads. "Why on earth there?"

"I'll fill you in on Saturday morning. It has to do with a death investigation."

It was nine o'clock on Saturday morning when Mark McClain parked his navy blue Beretta outside Vanessa's apartment. She had fresh coffee and muffins in the kitchen. As they sat at the table, he filled her in on the details of Phil Bentley's death.

"So how did he get from the motel to the lake?" she asked.

"Exactly!" Mark exclaimed. "How did he?"

"Hmm. Well, let's go look for some clues!" She grabbed her coat and headed for the door. Mark followed her grinning, sparked by her enthusiasm.

It was a cool but sunny day, a beautiful morning for a country drive. The roadside trees, unveiled of their leafy cloaks, exposed a wide view of the country farmland. An occasional barn rose up from the rolling, fenced pastures. They made the commute in under thirty minutes and easily found the Country Court Lodge, the only motel in Sprouses Corner. It was a single-story structure with a ground-level colonnade walkway along the front. The parking lot was graveled but neat. There was only one other vehicle in the lot at the lodge. They parked and walked into the office.

"I wonder if they rent rooms by the hour," whispered Vanessa as she hugged his arm. Mark smiled and thought, as vacant as it appeared, they would probably welcome any payments. He nudged her as the clerk approached the registration counter.

"Can I help you folks?" he asked. He was a slender, gray-haired white man with glasses and a mustache.

"Yes, sir. I hope so," said Mark. "I'm a reporter with *The News Progress* and we're following up on a missing person who was last seen here. He was Phil Bentley. He checked in on April 20, early in the morning."

"Oh, yeah. I heard they found his bones somewhere." He paused and gave them the once-over look before continuing. "Shirley was here that night. When I came in, his car was parked outside his room. The next morning, it was still there, in the exact same spot. He didn't answer the phone, so we checked his room. It was empty, so we called the police."

"Okay. Well, had he paid for the room?"

"Yeah. He used a credit card, was planning to stay one night."

"I see. I was hoping to show his picture to anyone who might have seen him."

"Well, I think Shirley's in the back. Wait here a minute." He returned with a dumpy lady with straight brown shoulder-length hair highlighted with streaks of gray. "Shirley, this is a reporter who's asking about Phil Bentley."

"Mark McClain, ma'am," responded the reporter.

"Yes. Wasn't that the strangest thing?" she said.

"Yes, ma'am. Strange." He handed her the picture faxed from the DMME. "Is this the man that checked in that morning?"

"Oh, no," she said immediately. "That man was a tall black man. And younger too. He said he left his ID in the car and was going to bring it in later."

"Are you sure?" asked Mark.

"I'm positive."

Mark and Vanessa exchanged glances and then turned to the motel attendants. "Thank you for your help," said Mark. "I may use this information in my article. By the way, do you know anything unusual about the Willis Mountain mine site? He was scheduled to visit it the next day. Anything suspicious there?"

"No, nothing I know about," answered the clerk.

"Well," Shirley interjected. "That family has been feuding over the mine company for years. I think they've filed a suit against the managers. Something about not dividing the profits fairly and not harvesting their timber because the directors go hunting in the woods there."

"Thank you, ma'am," said Mark. "We appreciate your openness and cooperation. If I have any more questions, can I give you a call?"

"Sure," answered the clerk as Shirley nodded.

Driving back to Farmville, Vanessa unleashed a regiment of questions.

"So Bentley never made the pivotal inspection at Willis Mountain," she said.

"No. Something happened before that," Mark answered.

"And the place he was last seen alive doesn't appear to be the motel," she said, reasoning. "Then, where was he last seen? Louisa?"

"No. He inspected a drilling site in Harrison County that afternoon. Supposedly, they were exploratory drilling for uranium. Dixie Mining, or something like that."

"Dixie Prospecting?" asked Vanessa.

"Yeah! Dixie Prospecting!" He turned and locked his gaze with Vanessa's. "You've heard of them?"

"Well, yes." She looked away but turned back and added, "They run the tungsten mine we toured."

Mark sensed she knew something else about them that she was withholding. "And ..." he probed.

"And, I just thought that was a coincidence." Vanessa smiled.

"Okay." Mark felt it was best to table the topic for now.

A t 5:25 in the evening, Dr. Hardy's office load had made him run past closing time, an all-too-frequent Friday occurrence. Mrs. Kent approached the check-out window. At age eighty-four, she was a small, slender white lady whose hair, with certain color enhancement, remained black. She still lived independently despite having early signs of Alzheimer's disease. Her past profession as a schoolteacher probably prompted her habit of bringing an apple to the doctor on each visit. Occasionally, the apple was not the freshest and this day's was a bit dowdy. Dr. Hardy just smiled, appreciative of her thoughtful gesture.

As Loren went to lock the door behind Mrs. Kent, Lucy approached Dr. Hardy. He looked up from his charting and saw that her eyes were sparkling.

"Did you hear what she just said?" she asked him with a smirk.

"No. What?"

"Loren told Mrs. Kent her next appointment date and she said 'Honey, you'd better write that down for me. My memory's about as long as my dick!'"

"No!" Dr. Hardy exclaimed.

"Yes! Cross my heart!" said Lucy.

"Yep, she did," Loren said, confirming the story. They all laughed solidly. "Oh," added Loren. "Greg left this at the front window." She handed him a manila envelope and a loose sheet of paper with typed print and a signature. Dr. Hardy read the paper.

"This is the certificate of occupancy," he said. "It means the house is finished!"

"Good," said Loren.

"So, he's all done?" asked Lucy.

"I suppose. Loren, did he ask to see me or anything?"

"Nope. He just walked up and kinda tossed that on the desk and left. He might have said 'Here you go,' like he's done before when he's left the monthly bills."

"That's odd," said Hardy.

"Weren't we supposed to have a final walk-through?" asked Lucy.

"Well, yeah. He had even mentioned it to me before. I guess I'll just give him a call."

That weekend, Dr. Hardy called his contractor.

"Greg, I got the certificate of occupancy you dropped off," he said. "Thanks."

"Yeah. I knew you were anxious to get the CO."

"When can we do the final walk-through?"

"What do you mean?"

"You said we would have a walk-through with all the subcontractors and you when we were done. When I have asked you questions, you deferred them to our 'final walk-through.'"

"Well," Greg paused briefly, and then posed. "Just what do you want to know?"

This is strange, thought Dr. Hardy. "Well, we need to know what maintenance we should perform on the well system and the geothermals. And, what electrical circuits and outlets are wired to the back-up generator. Also, what size generator will we need, and are you planning to wire in the driveway lights we bought?"

"The lights?" Another pause. "I'd forgotten all about them. I'll just get back to you, okay?"

"All right." Dr. Hardy had an ominous feeling about this.

It was nine o'clock when Dr. Hardy made it to his nursing home rounds for the week. The eldest residents were in bed by eight each evening, so Hardy selected patients that may still be up. Harrison Woods was a thirty-eight-year-old resident of Meadowview Terrace who was afflicted with cerebral palsy. He was a bed- and chair-ridden, obese black man with a speech impediment that hampered communication. By listening carefully, it was possible to understand most of his expressions. Dr. Hardy attributed his obesity to his inability to exercise along with his overindulgence in one of his few life pleasures—eating.

"Hello, Harrison," addressed Dr. Hardy. "Have you been having any problems?" Hardy noted a pungent, musky body odor, a unique trait of Harrison's.

"Yeth! Yeth!" Harrison answered excitedly. He spastically motioned to the hall with his arm. "Wit-tha! Wit-tha!"

"What? The window?" asked Hardy.

"Tha nurth! Wit-tha!"

"The nurse?"

"Yeth! Yeth!" Harrison nodded vigorously and repeated, "Wit-tha! Wit-tha!"

"He's trying to tell you that the nurse is a witch," explained Harrison's roommate.

"A nurse here? A witch?"

"Yeth! Yeth!" Harrison blurted.

"He thinks she placed a spell on him," the roommate said.

"A witch? Placed a spell?" Dr. Hardy looked from Harrison to his roommate and back.

"Yeth! Yeth! Uh huh."

"She's the blonde who works nights. Judy or Julie, I think," said his roommate.

"Okay, Harrison," said Dr. Hardy, assuredly. "I'll check into it. Don't you worry too much. I'll see about it." Hardy, however, was certain this wasn't covered in his Cecil's *Textbook of Medicine*.

"Kay," replied Harrison, smiling. "Kay."

Dr. Hardy realized that two nursing home reports of witchcraft were not a mere coincidence. He didn't accept the existence of witchcraft any more than he did wizardry or voodoo, but he had agreed to look into it. After signing his charts, he found a slender nurse at the medication cart. Her straw-colored hair was up in a bun, revealing her small, pixie-like ears with crescent-moon-shaped silver earrings. She had thin lips and pale blue eyes that twinkled.

"Hi, Dr. Hardy," she said. "You're late rounding this week."

"Yeah," he responded. He recognized her as Julie Newby, a nurse he had worked with before at the hospital. "Are you working the night shifts?"

"Yep. I'm a lady of the night now."

"I see. I was wondering, a few patients have reported a nurse was putting spells on them. Have you heard anything about that?"

"Sure." She leaned closer to him and whispered. "I practice a little witchcraft."

"No. I'm serious now."

"It's true! I've studied it for about three years now. My spells are simple but aimed at helping the patients—help with sleep, relieve pain, bowel regulation." She smiled, appearing proud.

"I see," said Dr. Hardy. It almost seemed reasonable. Maybe this was no more than a twist on homeopathy. "So, what kind of spell did you cast on Harrison?"

"Oh, Mr. Woods? For his odor!"

"Yeah. I've noticed that."

"The aids don't like to change his briefs. They avoid him, which makes it even worse!" She drew near to Dr. Hardy again and lowered her voice. "You see, he plays with himself all the time! It's just nasty!"

"You mean he masturbates?" asked Dr. Hardy. Maybe this was another of life's pleasures that Harrison had discovered.

"Yep." She squinted up her nose.

"Oh, okay." The doctor welcomed any assistance with this distasteful habit. "More power to you!"

"Well, it's new territory for me. I'm still trying different incantations to align his spiritual energies."

"All right. Well, thanks, Julie. And good luck with it." The enlightened physician turned down the hallway. Nurse Julie smiled and gave him a wink as they parted.

Chapter 12
Lost Hopes

The midday sky was a crisp blue with a few white wisps of clouds unfolding overhead as Dr. Hardy drove out onto the Clarksville Bridge. For a late February day, it seemed almost springlike. Dr. Hardy felt a budding anticipation of the sailing season awaken inside him. It might have been a pleasant afternoon for him except that, on his lunch break, he was hurrying out on an ME call. Even worse, it was on the opposite side of Buggs Island Lake, making for a formidable commute, certain to cause over an hour's delay in afternoon appointments. Just south of Clarksville, he turned off Route 15 onto Townsville Road. His progress was slowed by the twisting country road and by two slow-moving, twelve-wheeler cargo trucks in front of him.

The trucks were gray with white cabs, and their motors whined with the strain of their loads. The winding secondary road offered very little passing opportunity. As Hardy finally neared his destination, the trucks slowed even further to ease over a pothole in the road, swaying to the right and back to the left before leveling out again and gaining momentum. Dr. Hardy turned into the driveway where the Mecklenburg Life Saving ambulance and two county police cars were stationed.

The scene was a single-story residence with white siding and a small cinderblock front porch. Dr. Hardy approached the huddle of uniformed men beside the porch. A white sheet was spread over the three-tiered stairs to the stoop.

"This is Warren Chapman," said the on-scene detective, Bruce Duffer. "He is a forty-one-year-old man, the victim of a self-inflicted gunshot to the head. His mother and his sister left about 9 am to go to the store. They found him here when they returned about 10:45."

"Okay," said Dr. Hardy.

"He's suffered from depression and a longstanding back problem. Here's his medication list." Duffer handed Hardy a paper. It listed Zoloft, for depression, and pain medicines tramadol and gabapentin.

"He was a paramedic with Vance County," reported the Mecklenburg EMT, a short-haired tall woman. "But he's been disabled with his back. He hasn't worked since '04."

Duffer lifted the sheet to reveal a white male reclined upon the stairs. A shotgun was lying between his knees with the barrel pointing up. The detective carefully picked up the firearm as Dr. Hardy gloved up. "We've shot the photos. I'll tag this now. It's a twenty-gauge Browning shotgun."

"Thanks," stated Hardy. Duffer had done his job well. The doctor began his examination of Mr. Chapman, who leaned on his back against the cinderblock stairs. His neck was decimated from the blast and blood soaked his previously white shirt and khaki jacket. The back of his head was absent, its bloody bits splattered and stuck to the front of the house like wet gradoo. The face was intact but, lacking its bony support, laid limp like a rubber Halloween mask, eyes half-closed and gazing off in opposite directions. Dr. Hardy noted the body was still warm as he placed his thermometer in the right armpit, under the clothing. He found no signs of rigor mortis and the body temp was 94.2 degrees, indicating the time of death was two to three hours earlier.

"I estimate the time of death as about 10 a.m.," announced Dr. Hardy. The cause of death was certainly unmistakable. He looked at Detective Duffer. "Accidental, suicide, or homicide?"

"He left a note in the kitchen," said the detective, handing it to Dr. Hardy. It stated his chronic pain and debility as the factors driving this action and asked God and his family for forgiveness. "Apparently a suicide," he said.

"Okay," said Dr. Hardy. "I'll call it in to the Richmond office." His cell phone showed no signal. *Great*, he thought, *another delay.*

"We got a weak signal down by the road," the female EMT said, offering her assistance.

"Thanks!" The EMT was professional and composed. Hardy realized how hard it must be for a rescue worker to find a fellow EMS provider like this. He walked out to the road and dialed the OCME office from memory with a signal strength fluctuating between one and two bars. *What a place for an ME case*, he thought. *On a peninsula, accessed only by a North Carolina highway, in an area with no cell service.* He pictured his living patients arriving for their afternoon appointments and becoming disgruntled. Finally, he was able to present this case to the death investigator.

"Okay," said the investigator after hearing the details. "We can sign this out as a scene-visit viewing. An autopsy doesn't seem necessary. Can you draw the vitreous and blood samples?"

"Sure," agreed Dr. Hardy. The vitreous fluid of the eye is in an isolated body cavity, slow to decompose. It is valuable in analyzing chemistries and toxicology that would be corrupted quickly in the blood stream of a body. He walked back to the scene and assembled his syringes and tubes. As he transferred the clear eye fluid into a test tube he announced, "Okay. He can be taken to the funeral home now."

"No autopsy?" asked Detective Duffer.

"No. No autopsy," he said. As he dropped the specimens into his ME bag, Hardy heard a soft rumbling noise that was growing in intensity. It was a rattling sound from the street. Everyone turned to see the two gray cargo trucks barreling along to pass in front of the scene. The round, gold logos with the blue "DP" letters were painted on their sides. A loud clanking arose as each truck struck the pothole in the road.

"I wish they were moving that fast when I was stuck behind them!" said Hardy.

"They were probably loaded then," Duffer explained. "They're empty now."

"Dixie Prospecting," the EMT said. "They're from the tungsten mine."

"Oh," said Hardy. "Well, I'll see you all later." He went to his Jeep and set off in the wake of the trucks. As he drove, he thought,

Funny. The trucks were loaded going to the mine. It seems more logical to ship products out from the mine. Oh, well. Maybe they were just heading home for the day.

Dr. Hardy's office was, indeed, backed up upon his return. Lucy had triaged the patients and identified their primary problems to help focus the visits and had even written out some prescriptions. Dr. Hardy hated to rush visits, as some finer details of care often got neglected—preventive health screenings, lab results, or prescription refills. It took until six o'clock to wade through the load. Lucy left for home as the last patient exited, and Dr. Hardy found Alan Hancock leaning on the front desk counter with a sad smile.

"I heard you had to go out on the Chapman case, Doc," he said.

"Yeah. It's such a waste."

"I'd met him at the EMS symposium." Alan stared pensively at the floor. "I got some more news too."

"Bad or good?" Hardy sensed, however, that it wasn't good news.

"Bad. About our new squad building… the contractor's up and left."

"Greg Jackson? What do you mean?"

"Vanished! He shafted us on our last draw, about $30,000!"

"So, what does this mean?"

"We can't convert to a mortgage on an unfinished building. We can't finish it until we process the defaulted contractor. So, we're operating out of an abandoned oil truck garage with a new ambulance on the way!"

"What a damned mess!" Hardy exclaimed.

"And that's an understatement," Alan said.

After supper, Dr. Hardy shared the news about the missing Greg Jackson with Lucy.

"So, I guess our final walk-through is off," she said.

"It would appear so."

"What will we do about our financing?"

"Well, we got the CO, but the contractor has to sign off that there're no liens or outstanding debts for the mortgage company to accept the loan."

"Have we paid him his final bill?" she asked.

"No. I asked the bank to hold payment, since he hadn't credited us back our down payment. And there're some discrepancy items to address too. The bank suggested placing the payment in an escrow account. That way the money would be available to him, pending verification. It will release all builders' liens but hold back payment until both parties come to a settlement. I'll call him once the escrow is funded."

The bank called Dr. Hardy the next day just before noon. The escrow funding was complete, although Dr. Hardy had to provide $35,000 by a credit card advance to cover the uncredited, hence double-billed, deposit. A confirmation was faxed to his office.

"So it's all done?" asked Lucy.

"It looks like it." He showed her the fax. "Now I can call Greg about our walk-through."

"Put it on speaker phone!" Lucy urged as he dialed.

"Okay." The phone rang and immediately went to voicemail.

A machine-like female voice stated, "The subscriber's voicemail box is full and cannot accept further messages. Please try again later." Lucy and Dr. Hardy looked at each other, speechless.

About four in the afternoon, a Mecklenburg County deputy entered the office. Loren led him into the back hallway. Dr. Hardy met him there, assuming it was some detail regarding the suicide.

"Dr. Hardy," the deputy said, handing Hardy a white paper. "This is a notification. You've been served."

"Oh, thanks," he said, sarcastically. As the deputy retreated, Lucy peered curiously around her spouse.

"What is it?" she pried.

"It's a mechanic's lien on our new house!"

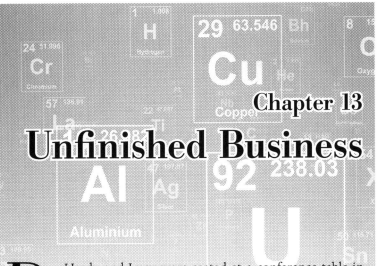

Chapter 13
Unfinished Business

Dr. Hardy and Lucy were seated at a conference table in the office of attorney Jonathan Bancroft. Hardy noted the smell was like that of a library, which was only natural since one wall was lined by shelves filled with legal textbooks.

"Since we set up an escrow," Bancroft said, "there can be no mechanic's lien. In fact, your escrow was funded four hours before he filed the lien. His lien is worthless."

"So we don't have to worry about losing the house?" said Lucy.

"Absolutely not!"

"So where do we go from here?" asked Dr. Hardy.

"Either you can reach an agreement, seek arbitration, or go to court. You've anted up your money. It's really up to him to show proof of debt."

"I hear that he has disappeared. What if we don't hear back from him?" Hardy continued.

"Well, the escrow will stay for two years. If he doesn't ask for resolution, it reverts back to you, with interest."

Lucy gave a small smile to Dr. Hardy. "I had a bad feeling about him. You should have gotten other bids like I suggested." Hardy realized the gentlemen's handshake agreement between "good ole boys" had been a bit idealistic. However, getting additional bids hadn't protected the rescue squad from this either.

"Well, let me know when you hear from him," Bancroft concluded.

"Okay. We will. Thanks," said Dr. Hardy.

"I hope it's after two years!" said Lucy.

Mark McClain was at *The News Progress* office Friday afternoon when Vanessa Foster came in. Basketball season had passed and spring soccer and baseball seasons had not yet begun. They could possibly have an evening to themselves.

"I've got you an ad to run," she announced, smiling. "Full page, color!"

Mark had run ads she had brought before for the Dixie Prospecting uranium project. He had tried to remain neutral on the uranium mining issue, but radiation scared him. She had never revealed why she was their courier, but the e-payments or checks always listed "Foster Marketing" as the source. He assumed her business communications work included advertising and marketing for some firms.

"Okay. Great," he said smiling.

"Can we go somewhere private when you're done working?" she asked provocatively.

"Sure," he answered. "Ah... just let me close up a few things. How about if I get us a pizza, and we meet at my place?"

"That'd be great."

"All right. About forty-five minutes to an hour?"

"Okay," she kissed his cheek. "I'll meet you there then."

Mark arrived with a Gino's pepperoni pizza and produced two cold bottles of Michelob Light from the fridge. They sat at his kitchen table and relaxed.

"So, any new developments in the Bentley case?" asked Vanessa.

"I'm afraid not. It's still a mystery to me." Mark felt that Vanessa was also still a mystery to him. He studied her features as she chewed a bite of pizza. Gosh, she was pretty! "So what do you feel like tonight?" He felt her foot, below the table, creeping up his pant leg.

"I don't know," she said smiling. "But I feel like showering after a day's work. Care to join me?"

"Well, I am feeling kinda dirty, now that you mention it." She laughed and walked off into the bedroom.

"I hope your water's running hot."

Mark accompanied Alan Hancock to the Mecklenburg County sheriff's office to meet with investigators. The department was in a newly renovated, abandoned pajama factory, an upgrade from the dingy, cramped modular building adjoining the old jail. They sat at a wooden table in a conference-type briefing room with detectives Bruce Duffer and Carl Wilborn. Wilborn was a tall, middle-aged man with short-clipped graying hair.

"Both Carl Wilborn and I are working on the Greg Jackson case," Bruce Duffer began. "We've filed criminal charges of contractor fraud, and Carl has been focused on locating Mr. Jackson."

"He used a credit card in Georgia ten days ago," said Carl. "I've spoken to some of his former workers. They said he had mentioned high-paying contractors' jobs in Florida in the aftermath of Hurricane Bill and Tropical Storm Claudette. We think he fled there looking for another quick buck."

"How will you find him in Florida?" asked Alan.

"We've contacted the Florida state police," said Wilborn. "They have our arrest warrant."

"So, we just wait?" Alan said.

"Well, yes, but we've alerted them to look out for stray contractors," Carl added.

As they stood to leave, Mark addressed Detective Duffer. "Oh, Bruce?"

"Yeah."

"Any breaks on the Bentley bones case?" he inquired.

"No. Last seen at the motel on April 20."

"How'd you determine that?" Mark said, probing.

"From the Buckingham County police. It was out of our jurisdiction and they went to the motel."

"Oh? Well, so did I. I showed the desk clerk Phil Bentley's picture. The man who checked in was *not* Phil Bentley."

"What are you saying?" asked a concerned Duffer.

"It was a black man who checked in under his name. And Bentley had made his afternoon visit to the uranium drill site in Harrison.

He was due at the kyanite mine the next day. And the mine was in jeopardy from some mining violations."

"Really? If this is right, we will need an expanded jurisdiction for the investigation. Maybe state police or even FBI."

B oydton Life Station held their March business meeting at the old oil truck garage again. Alan Hancock updated the members on the new squad building construction.

"Hence, we have a freeze placed on the construction project until the criminal case is resolved. It looks like this place is our home for now."

"So can't we get someone to finish it?" asked a member.

"Nope. We just have to sit on it."

"I move that we take out a contract on the contractor!" a member called out. This was received with a wave of supportive murmuring and laughter.

"Well, on a positive note," Hancock continued, "our new ambulance will arrive Friday!"

"What will we call it?" asked Buddy McClain.

"Well, we have Units 11 and 12 now. Until we sell Unit 11, it will be a back-up ambulance. I guess it will be Unit 13."

"Thirteen? That's an unlucky number!" said Della.

"And, arriving on Friday, Unit 13!" added another member.

"All right," said Alan. "We need to preserve our teen numbers for future expansions, assuming we still have a future. And, I've already applied to the county EMS for the Unit 13 designation. You all know this bad luck superstition is just nonsense!"

"Look around you. See where we're meeting? Is this good luck?" Della asked.

Some low volume, undertoned chatter ensued, ending in a weakly positive consensus.

"If there is no further business, everyone is welcome to come by Friday afternoon and welcome our new ambulance, Unit 13. Meeting adjourned!"

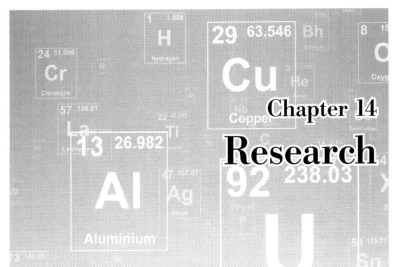

"Ethanol Plant Denied Permit" was the front-page headline of *The News Progress*. Chase City mayor Ralph Rogers had attended the county board of supervisors meeting and requested they not grant a zoning permit for ethanol production. He presented the petitions that the Association to Preserve Mecklenburg had circulated, filled with hundreds of signatures of concerned, registered voters. The local politicians hesitantly conceded to his campaign. Except for a family winery on Lake Gaston, the only commercial alcohol brewed in Mecklenburg County would be bootleg.

Mark received a call from Vanessa Foster after she had read the article. "I'm kind of sad that Chase City didn't get the ethanol plant," she said.

"Yeah, me too. I was hoping for some area development here," Mark responded.

"I suppose this is a victory for the Association to Preserve Mecklenburg."

"I guess you're right. Oh, did you see your ad?"

"Yes, I did. It was excellent." She then added, "I suppose the association will have to find a new cause to pursue."

"Maybe uranium mining?" posed Mark.

"I guess," she said flatly. Then she abruptly changed the subject. "Oh! Our annual science fair is in three weeks, April 21. It might make a good public interest story for the *Progress*."

"Yeah." Mark perceived her avoidance of the uranium issue. It seemed so unlike her. "Kind of like the tungsten mine tour. Will you be there?"

"Of course."

"It's sounding even more interesting. I'll put it on my schedule." Remembering their previous fall excursion, he had an idea. "Hey. What if SVCC toured the kyanite mine this year instead of the tungsten mine? We might get to snoop around some! That was where Phil Bentley was scheduled to go."

"Yeah! That might prove to be revealing. We can talk to James Callahan about that at the science fair."

"Okay, then."

Later, McClain drove over to the sheriff's department to retrieve the weekly county legal filings, always looking for a scoop. He had called ahead to coordinate his visit with Bruce Duffer's availability. He was able to meet with the detective at his cubicle.

"Any news on the contractor, Greg Jackson?" asked Mark.

"Actually, yes," answered Duffer. He kept his professional persona as he continued. "He was arrested in Lakeland, Florida, outside of a hardware store. He was buying building supplies."

"That's great!" Mark knew the problem was still far from resolved. "How will he be prosecuted?"

"He'll need extradition to Virginia, which can be an involved process."

"Who does that?"

"Carl Wilborn has contacted the FBI. They have a fugitive division that specializes in extradition of criminals."

"How long is this process?" Mark feared the prosecution would grow stagnant.

"I can't say. Anywhere from two days to two months."

"Where will he end up?"

"In the Mecklenburg County jail. He'll be charged and, if bail is set, could be released until trial. Since he is a proven flight risk, there may be no bail set or it might be extremely high. He does face felony charges."

"I see." Mark realized this was his scoop. "Can I print about the arrest?"

"Sure. The other details will have to wait." Mark was fine with that. He was delighted to have some good news to report.

D r. Hardy and Lucy drove their daughters to the governor's school science fair at the John H. Daniel campus of SVCC. They set out from Dr. Hardy's office at five thirty since Vikki needed to arrive thirty minutes before the start of the event.

"So what's this going to be like?" asked Dr. Hardy.

"Well," began Vikki, bubbling with enthusiasm, "we will present our projects and then parents and friends can visit our exhibits. They can have refreshments, ask questions, and all that stuff."

"Sounds good," commented Lucy. "Maybe Anna will be there next year."

"Yeah, sure," replied Anna flatly, as she gazed out of her window. Dr. Hardy glanced at Lucy with a wry smile.

The campus was several single-story brick buildings connected by sidewalks. The first building was taller than the others, housing the gym-atorium, the site of the fair. There was a crowd of sixty to seventy-five guests seated in the folding chairs facing the stage. James Callahan hosted the program, introducing each of the six experiments carried out by the four-student lab groups. One project studied the effect of alternating saline concentrations on the viability of hydrae. Another compared the productivity of hydroponically cultivated bean sprouts with that of soil rooting. Vikki's group had monitored skin pH and electrical conductivity of subjects using four different dermatologic moisturizers over a six week course. Their results included photos of the test subjects' thighs at the beginning and end of the treatment period. Dr. Hardy was impressed by the caliber of these investigations.

"Our final project involved the entire science class with every student contributing to it," announced Callahan. "I'm proud of the work they have all done in their individual groups as well as this joint project. The students took a three-day radon sampling from their homes, and we plotted the results geographically. Anyway, I'll let the researchers present their data."

Keith Lawson explained how radon gas emanates from rocks that have high uranium content, such as granite, shale, and limestone. It seeps into basements of houses and is felt to be responsible for the 13 percent of lung cancers that develop in nonsmokers. Vikki gave details about the test procedures and explained that the widely fluctuating levels made prolonged sampling necessary. Andy Francis interpreted the slides that showed the columns of readings, a scatter diagram of results per zip codes, and finally the map with the colored pins.

"In conclusion," said Andy, "there are no significant variations in radon concentrations among the four counties sampled in this study. Of note was that only two readings were above 3 pico-Curies. Although both of these were in Harrison County, the p value was only 0.29, not statistically significant."

Dr. Hardy understood research statistics and knew scientific conclusions sought p values of 0.05 or less, meaning there was less than a 5 percent chance that the results were attributable to random variations in sampling. This meant that the chance that this study actually found a real difference in the Harrison readings was still 71 percent. This left him feeling an element of doubt, only a bit reassured by the absence of elevated readings in his own county. These students, still just in high school, had completed projects worthy of advanced collegiate programs. The SVCC science department had displayed an unexpectedly impressive level of education for a rural community college. Seeing that his daughter had done a medically related study made him swell with pride.

Vikki Hardy stood beside her project display after the presentations. Holding a cup of punch, Dr. Hardy found pleasure in studying the photos. Mark McClain snapped a picture of him at the exhibit and remarked, "Nice job!"

"Thanks!" answered Vikki.

Dr. Hardy followed Mark over to where James Callahan stood, Vanessa at his side. He addressed Callahan with praise. "This program was excellent!"

"Thank you," Callahan said. "You're Vikki's dad?"

"Yes. Obie Hardy."

"The doctor?"

"Yes, that's me. I guess I'm still a bit of a science geek. These projects were quite advanced. I'm impressed by the caliber of work your community college has produced."

"Thanks. I try to evoke the kids' interest."

"Yeah," Vanessa added. "The tungsten mine tour was a big hit last fall."

"Oh, yeah. Vikki raved about it!" said Hardy.

"I'd like to see the class tour the kyanite mine this fall," said Vanessa.

"The kyanite mine?" said Callahan.

"That's at Willis Mountain, right?" said Hardy.

"Yeah!" answered Vanessa. "It's about the same distance away. It might be good to see another type of mining operation."

"Sounds like a good idea," Callahan said. "I'll look into it. Maybe alternate sites each year. It would give us a change in routine."

As Dr. Hardy wandered off, Mark McClain joined him. "You know what, Dr. Hardy?" he said.

"What?"

"Do you remember the bones found on the beach in Buffalo Junction?"

"Yeah. ID'd as Bentley, right?"

"Right. He was scheduled to inspect the kyanite mine the morning he disappeared."

"Oh, no kidding? So, the plot thickens. Do you know anything about that mine?"

"They were in jeopardy of closing, due to some regulation violations."

Hardy shared a sobering look with McClain.

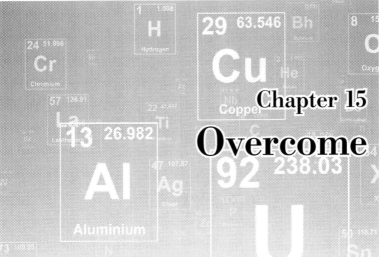

Chapter 15
Overcome

G ary Dalton was a black septuagenarian scheduled for a routine follow-up in Dr. Hardy's office. His speech was impaired from a past stroke that also damaged his thalamus, the emotional regulator of the brain. His right leg weakness created a perceptible shuffle in his gait, and he wielded a cane for stability. Dr. Hardy noted he was overdue for measuring his cholesterol and kidney function. He tried to limit Dalton's blood tests to two or three times a year due to his exaggerated fear reaction to needle sticks. His volatile emotions were the result of his damaged thalamus.

"Mr. Dalton, we need to check your cholesterol today," announced Dr. Hardy.

"Naw!" said Mr. Dalton. "Really?" His vocal communication was limited to single words or short phrases.

"Yeah. I'm afraid so." Hardy smiled understandingly. Experience had taught him not to inform Dalton of venipunctures before the staff took his vital signs as his profuse sweating had soaked the blood pressure cuff before.

"Aw right," he said with a nervous chuckle.

Dr. Hardy stepped out of the exam room and found Lucy in the hall. "I need labs drawn in room 2," as if it were any routine venipuncture.

"Okay," she said. "Oh, room 1 is finishing her nebulizer treatment now."

"All right. I'll get it. Thanks."

Dr. Hardy found Jean Pittard in room 1, sitting on the exam table with the nebulizer mouthpiece in her mouth. The machine was still running, but the vaporized bronchodilator flow had ceased. Janice was taking deep breaths. Hardy shut off the machine.

"Looks like you sucked this one dry, Ms. Pittard," he said. "Did that help your congestion?"

"Huh?" she answered sleepily. "Uh huh." The doctor listened to her chest to confirm the lung wheezing had resolved.

"Here's a prescription for an inhaler and an antibiotic." He handed her the scripts.

"Ah… thanks," she responded mechanically, her eyes glassy.

Dr. Hardy met Lucy in the hallway again.

"Gary Dalton," she said, shaking her head and smiling. "Poor thing! I've never seen anyone laugh and cry at the same time! He was soaked with sweat and tears a-flowing."

Janice Pittard emerged from the exam room behind Dr. Hardy and, with a blank gaze, turned up the hallway. Lucy noticed that she appeared lost.

"Janice," she said. "Turn around. If you're leaving, the other way is out."

"Oh… yeah," she said flatly and changed directions. As she continued across the waiting room, Loren, who had begun cleaning the exam room, called out to her.

"Janice! You forgot your purse!" She carried it out to her. "Here."

"Oh…thanks." She dreamily progressed out to her car.

"What's up with her?" Lucy asked. "She's in a trance."

"She was hyperventilating during her treatment," Dr. Hardy concluded. "She's probably light-headed."

"Light-headed? She's in another world!"

Mr. Dalton was now passing them in the hall. He had a Band-Aid on his arm and appeared as if he had been caught in a spring shower. His balding scalp was beaded with perspiration and his shirt clung to his torso. He chuckled a little as he headed to the front door.

Alan Hancock approached the registration window as Loren

locked the front doors. He was grinning as he held out two slips of paper in his hand.

"I think your patient dropped her prescriptions," he said.

"Oh, that was Janice," Loren said. "I'll take them and call them in for her."

"What are you doing to your patients, Doc?" Alan asked. "I passed a zombie in the parking lot, then a man looking like he was in heroin withdrawal!"

"It's a long story," Hardy responded smiling.

"Well, I've got some good news."

"It's about time. What is it?"

"Greg Jackson is in the Boydton jail!"

"Really? It sounded like it was going to take a while. Good."

"The FBI fugitive squad snatched him up."

"So, he hasn't made bail yet, has he?"

"Not that I know of. He just got in here last night."

"Well, that's great news!"

The following Wednesday, Dr. Hardy had finished his morning appointments by one fifteen and began reviewing lab results and phone messages. Thus began his afternoon "off." His paper shuffle was soon interrupted by an ME call.

"Well, just another chore for my half day off," he told Lucy sarcastically as he left the office.

"Where is it?" she asked.

"On the other side of the lake, near Ivy Hill."

That particular area of Buggs Island Lake was fairly secluded and had always appealed to Dr. Hardy. Local high school students found it an inviting make-out site since Virginia police had to drive through North Carolina to reach it. It was understandably less heavily patrolled by law officers. That was not the case this day, however, as he found three county cruisers at the site as well as the brown "dive team" truck.

It was a sunny afternoon in the last week of May, a perfect time to be off work. The pale green colors of the spring foliage were just giving in to the deeper, shady hues of the summer. Several lake cottages populated a cul-de-sac off of Ivy Hill Road. Bruce met Dr. Hardy in the driveway of a small, one-story house with a screened porch.

"The dive team recovered the body about 1:22," he said in his businesslike manner. "Apparently, she was floating on a raft and slipped off in about ten feet of water. She's a seventeen-year-old non-swimmer."

"When was that?" asked Dr. Hardy.

"About 11:45."

"Seventeen? She wasn't in school?"

"Senior skip day. She would have graduated in June. She was here with her cousin swimming."

Dr. Hardy felt his heart sink. Vikki was graduating this June! This could be her classmate! "What's her name?"

"Jolanda White, birth date 10-24-92," reported Duffer. "She's in the boat back here with Deputy Turner from the dive team."

The white fiberglass skiff was beached behind the house. A sheet covered a human-shaped form on the floor, guarded by a man in a black wetsuit.

"Dr. Hardy," said the diver. "We found her in eleven feet of water. She'd been submerged over ninety minutes."

Dr. Hardy pulled the sheet aside to expose the lifeless youth. Jolanda, a light-complexioned black female, lay face up. Her skin was smooth and clear, not littered by piercings or tattoos. She wore a white-and-aqua bikini, which fit her perfectly, accentuating her figure. He manipulated her neck and pressed on her ribs, assessing her body for fractures. She was still limber and warm to touch, not yet gripped with rigor mortis. Dr. Hardy had an eerie feeling, like he was somehow violating an unconscious female instead of just probing a corpse. The axillary temperature read ninety degrees.

"I'll call this in to Richmond. You said her cousin witnessed the drowning?" Hardy asked.

"Yes," Duffer answered. "Will they need an autopsy?"

"I doubt it. I'll still need blood for alcohol and toxicologies." He shook his head sadly as Deputy Turner recovered her with the sheet.

"She was a basketball player," added Detective Duffer.

"It's such a shame."

Hardy sat in his Jeep to write up the CME-1 form and call his report to the Office of the Chief Medical Examiner, OCME. It was determined an autopsy was unnecessary and Dr. Hardy returned to the boat to obtain the body fluid samples.

"Tell the funeral home I'll sign the death certificate," Hardy told Duffer.

"Sure. And thanks, Doc."

Dr. Hardy started home and met the Freemans Funeral Home hearse passing him in the opposite lane. This was a common occurrence when leaving death scenes. He stopped at the intersection of Townsville Road and paused for approaching traffic. It was the pair of Dixie Prospecting trucks, lollygagging toward Townsville.

"Good! At least I won't be stuck behind them again," he thought aloud. Today, however, it wouldn't have mattered. Dr. Hardy felt like time was suspended, like the world had stopped when this teenager's life had. When he crossed back into Virginia on Route 15, the surrealistic fog began clearing and he dialed his wife.

"The ME case was a high school girl," he said solemnly.

"Oh no! A Bluestone student?" asked Lucy.

"I think so. A senior, Jolanda White."

"She'd be in Vikki's class!" exclaimed Lucy. "Oh, my God! That's awful!"

"Is she home yet?"

"She should be in twenty or thirty minutes."

"I'll see you in a few minutes. Love you!" said Dr. Hardy.

Dr. Hardy and Lucy were in the kitchen when Vikki and Anna came through the door. Vikki's eyes were puffy and cheeks pink from crying.

"Mom... Dad..." she said weakly, and sniffed, letting her backpack fall to the floor. Dr. Hardy took her in his arms, overcome by the urge to comfort his daughter.

"I know," he said as her eyes filled again with tears. Lucy embraced Anna, who was standing in a numbed silence. She was in blue jeans with a black T-shirt and boots. Her tough, biker-type façade melted as the waves of adolescent female emotion engulfed her as well.

Photo courtesy of *The News Progress*

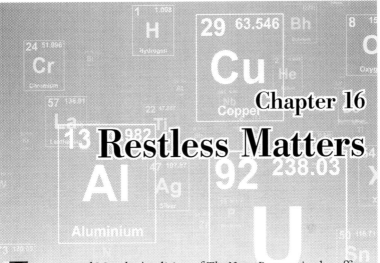

Chapter 16
Restless Matters

L ucy read Monday's edition of *The News Progress* in the office kitchen during lunch break.

"Jolanda White is the headlined story," she said. "She was an honor roll student and an athlete, accepted to Longwood College."

"It's a terrible shame," stated Dr. Hardy. "She was a pretty girl too."

"They held a memorial service at Bluestone Friday," said Lucy, turning the page and taking a bite of pizza. "Oh. The Clarksville Wine Festival is this week, Memorial Day weekend."

"Well, that's something positive! I think I could use a glass of wine myself."

Loren came into the kitchen holding some folded papers. "A deputy just delivered this for y'all," she explained, handing Dr. Hardy the papers.

"What?" he said as he began reading.

"What is it?" asked Lucy.

"It's Greg Jackson. He's filed an action to enforce the mechanics lien!"

"Greg Jackson? I thought he was locked up," Lucy said.

"I guess his lawyer filed it. He's moving to foreclose on our house!"

"Can he do that?" asked Lucy, anxiously.

"Bancroft said he couldn't. We need to let him know about

this." He trusted the assurance Bancroft had given them but still felt a need for reaffirmation. "We need to call him today!"

"I'll do it," said Lucy.

"Oh," Dr. Hardy added. "He's notified the adjacent property owners, Mrs. Smith and the Macklins' farm. I wonder what they'll think of this."

It was after four before John Bancroft's greatly anticipated return phone call. Dr. Hardy and Lucy both listened on different extensions.

"You're perfectly safe," he said. "All of the funds are in escrow. This action is absolutely worthless to them."

"Well, what about them notifying our neighbors? That makes us look shabby!" said Lucy.

"That part is just ruthless and mean! They're just trying to tarnish your images. I'll remind the court of the escrow account and ask to have the motion squashed."

"Thanks," said Hardy as he shared a serious look with his wife.

"Oh. Does he still have a key to your house?" asked Bancroft.

"Yes, he does," said Lucy.

"Well, you need to get the locks changed, just as a precaution."

That entire week the Hardys spent most of their after-work hours moving items to their new home. They saved the beds and TV for Saturday, their anticipated first night in the house. By noon on Saturday, they had transported the master bed and the two kids' beds, along with mattresses and foundations. All that remained for provisional living was assembling the beds and the TV service hook-up. Dr. Hardy kneeled on the floor beside his tool bag, aligning the corners of a bed frame. His cell phone interrupted him. A nurse from Meadowview Terrace nursing home reported that Carolyn Schimdt had been found dead in her bed. She had a prearranged after-death plan that called for a cremation to be done.

"How about taking a break?" suggested Dr. Hardy. He knew Lucy would not rest until the house was in order.

"Well, okay," she agreed reluctantly. Dr. Hardy figured she must be hungry.

"How about riding over to Clarksville? We could check out the wine festival," he said.

"Can we eat at Subway?" asked Vikki.

"Sure," said Hardy.

They went first to Subway, where Dr. Hardy gave his daughters some cash.

"You girls go eat and then hang out. Dad and I will meet you at the Presbyterian Church parking lot in about an hour," said Lucy.

"We'll probably check out some of the wine booths," added Dad.

"Okay. Thanks," said Vikki as she bounded off with Anna.

Dr. Hardy and Lucy stopped by Walker's Funeral Home for him to sign the cremation certificate on his nursing home patient. Seeing her body reminded him of the analogy she had made about God's waiting room.

"I guess He called for her," Hardy thought out loud.

"Yes. It was her time," said Maxwell Walker, the funeral director.

"She was a fascinating woman, right up till the end."

Mr. Walker placed the lid on her cardboard casket, not much more than a giant shoe-box, and slid her into the cremation furnace. Dr. Hardy shed his gloves, washed his hands, and signed the form.

"Thanks, Dr. Hardy," said Walker ever so politely.

"Sure. Anytime."

Dr. Hardy rejoined Lucy in the back vestibule of the funeral home.

"So that's number two," she said. "Mama said deaths always come in threes."

"Yeah. I've heard that, too." Trying to salvage the rest of their day, he added, "Let's go get some wine!"

"Okay. But they had better have crab dip!"

The weather was ideal for Clarksville's fourth annual Wine Festival: a few clouds and eighty-two degrees. Tents covered the tables of the twelve vendors representing area wineries and restaurants. The Hardys got their official event wine-sampling glasses from the admissions table and wandered about the spread. They tasted two white wines from Rosemont Vineyards before Lucy targeted the Cooper's Landing table.

"O-o-oh! Cooper's crab dip!"

It was a local restaurant favorite of theirs, so they bought a serving of the appetizer. Adorned with bread slices for dipping or spreading, today's plate was as delightful as ever.

"I'll just make a meal of this!" said Lucy after her first bite.

"That's fine by me."

They were enjoying a sweet "after dip" muscadine wine from Dublin, North Carolina, when Lucy suddenly froze. Her gaze was fixed on something or someone. Obie Hardy looked in the direction of her stare and saw a familiar appearing form.

"Is that Greg Jackson?" she asked incredulously.

"I think it is!" responded Hardy.

"Isn't he supposed to be in jail?"

He abruptly looked their way, head and shoulders wavering some. Pointing a finger at them, he yelled out. "Hey!"

Obie touched Lucy's arm and turned her away from him. "Let's go find the kids," he suggested.

As they walked away, they heard Greg holler again. It sounded a little slurred and was muffled by the drone of the crowd, but it seemed like he shouted, "Deadbeats!"

On the drive home, Lucy said in speculation, "I wonder how Greg got out to come there."

"I don't know," answered Dr. Hardy. "Maybe he made bail or even got out on work release."

At their new home, the Hardys had a tranquil night, largely due to the lack of established TV service. They were able, nonetheless, to watch *The Hangover* on DVD. It was a bit risqué for their teenagers, but it was taken in the context of comic entertainment. The house was quiet, being a half mile from the nearest country road. Vikki, however, still complained of the whippoorwill whose incessant callings kept her awake.

It was Sunday, their second night, when Lucy nudged Obie Hardy in bed.

"Did you hear that?" she whispered.

"No," he answered groggily.

"Something bumped upstairs." She looked up at the ceiling and then at Obie. "Go see what it was." He knew she would not let him rest until she was assured that all was in order. He climbed out of their reassembled bed and trudged out of the bedroom.

Upon entering the family room, he noticed a light was visible from over the loft, back where the unfinished bonus room was, directly above his bedroom. *That's odd,* he thought as he climbed the stairs to investigate. All was in order, no intruders seen. He switched off the light and retreated. *The switch had been left on,* he surmised, *with a probable loose lightbulb. It could come on if something had just jarred the wall. Surely, it was just the house settling.* His daughters remained asleep upstairs, despite the nearby sound of a whippoorwill.

"What was it?" inquired Lucy curiously.

"Nothing. An upstairs light was left on," he answered. He realized that this did not explain the noise but hoped she would be satisfied if he reported a positive discovery.

"Oh," she said. The bedside digital clock displayed 12:23 as he returned to his bed.

Monday was Memorial Day and the office was closed. Dr. Hardy was still in bed when the phone rang at 6:45.

"This is the ME's office for Dr. Hardy."

"Yes. This is Dr. Hardy," he said.

"We have a prisoner death at the hospital in South Hill. Can you take the case?"

"Sure. I'm going there for rounds now anyway."

"Great. The body is in the morgue. The name's Greg Jackson."

"Greg Jackson?" he exclaimed. Lucy sprang up in bed.

"Yeah. Greg Jackson. Forty-eight-year-old male. Okay?"

"Okay, sure. I'll do it." Dr. Hardy looked at his wife.

"Greg died?" she asked, wide-eyed.

"Yeah," said Dr. Hardy solemnly.

"What happened?"

"I don't know, but I guess I'll find out."

"That's number three." Lucy spoke as if a prophecy was fulfilled.

Dr. Hardy opened the hospital morgue refrigerator and rolled out the body on the stainless steel tray. Unzipping the body bag exposed the corpse of Greg Jackson, his wayward house contractor. Mucous and emesis were matted in his black mustache and his face was a purplish hue. A plastic endotracheal tube still protruded from his mouth. This was, unmistakably, the man who had pointed at him disparagingly just two days earlier. His eyes were bloodshot and his tongue showed bite marks along both sides. Aside from the IV punctures and electrical burns to the chest, the wounds of resuscitation, there were no signs of life-threatening injuries. It appeared this death would require an autopsy.

Dr. Hardy reviewed the medical records that accompanied the body in the morgue. Greg had suffered a full arrest, cardiopulmonary failure, prior to arrival in the ER. Resuscitative measures had been futile. *Yep*, he thought. *This one needs a post.* He read Alan Hancock's name on the EMS printout. He could probably get the scoop on this case from him. On the way out, he commandeered the ER blood samples drawn from Jackson to send to the ME's central office.

Driving back to Boydton, he noticed some vehicles at the BLS outpost site and pulled in. He found Alan Hancock in the office with a mug of coffee. As he had anticipated, Alan had no loss of words regarding the event.

"Doc," he began, "we got this call from the jail. A forty-eight-year-old male who was twitching and hallucinating, seeing spiders crawling everywhere. So, we get to the scene and find Greg Jackson, our fraudulent contractor. It was our charges that had put him in jail! Needless to say, this completely freaked him out. It was like he was in DTs!"

"I saw him at the wine festival Saturday."

"Yeah. He was in some sort of work release program, they said."

"He looked drunk then."

"Uh-huh. Maybe it was DTs then. He was as wild as an animal! He was screaming, fighting, and agitated. A deputy rode with us to help restrain him. We did manage to get an IV in him somehow. Then, just about at Big Fork, he puked and started seizing. He bit his tongue and pulled out his IV; puke and blood were flying everywhere! His O2 sat dropped to 66 percent. The monitors went crazy! His BP read 66 and his heart rate read 66. Then, he stopped breathing. We were just five minutes out from South Hill ER, so we just suctioned him and bagged him all the way there. They coded him for twenty minutes!"

"It sounds awful."

"Trust me, it was! We've christened Unit 13 now. It took a half hour to clean the back." Hancock's eyes twinkled with the excitement of reliving the squad call.

"I sent him up for an autopsy. Anyway, I guess he'll never pay you back for the construction fraud," Hardy speculated.

"I reckon not. Unless he had good life insurance."

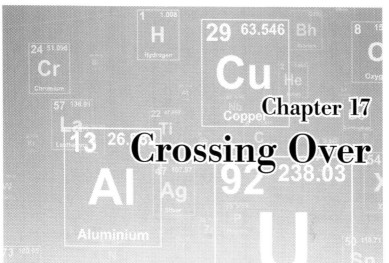

Chapter 17
Crossing Over

The Clarksville bypass bridge traversing Buggs Island Lake was part of the Route 58 Corridor Development Program initiated in 1989. The program's goal was to expand most of Virginia's longest highway to four lanes. The Clarksville bypass alone cost $75 million and took over three years to complete. The bridge span was nearly a mile long and rose sixty feet above the water. This dedication and grand opening of the bridge bypass was forecast as a much celebrated event. Mark McClain found himself among the crowd of about four hundred who gathered at the overlook area east of the town.

The Clarksville mayor introduced the state's secretary of transportation, whose comments preceded the governor's speech. The Virginia governor, Dwight Carpenter, dedicated the bridge to the late Judge John Tisdale. Mark strained to get photos of the more prominent officials, including the lieutenant governor and Senator Sidney Francis. Occoneechee State Park, on the lake at the foot of the bridge, provided ice cream and lemonade to the spectators. In the wake of the recent drowning, this positive event lifted Mark's spirits. This lake community was, indeed, a jewel.

Historically, the lake's waters formed a geographic riparian barrier, dividing the county and alienating nearby communities. The slow-moving ferry was eventually replaced by a toll bridge and, now, by this modern roadway. Once an obstacle to land travel, Buggs Island Lake had blossomed into a most precious asset of Mecklenburg County. It boasted a hydroelectric power plant, regionally renowned bass fishing, and a reservoir that supplied water as far away as Henderson, North Carolina, and Virginia Beach, 140 miles to the east.

The Tisdale Bridge opened to bicycle and foot traffic after the ceremony as, in the future, only motorized vehicles would be allowed. From the apex, Mark photographed the lake-scape, spreading out for miles. The Goat Island bend was visible four miles to the east, blocking the view of Ivy Hill just distantly. He had been concerned that the new highway would pollute the natural scenery, but this was more than compensated for by the impressive sights from the overpass. His appreciation of this treasure was strengthened, and he found himself grateful for the efforts of the Association to Preserve Mecklenburg. The ethanol plant idea had seemed to pose little threat, unlike a uranium mining mishap, which could create widespread, irreversible devastation.

M elody Manor was Boydton's assisted living facility, an old motel that had been converted to a rest home. It was a one-story brick structure in a U shape with a covered walkway along the inside border. Alan Hancock and Buddy McClain answered an EMS call to the site. It was for an elderly female with shortness of breath who became fairly comfortable once oxygen had been started. The responders rolled their patient into the back of the new BLS Unit 13 for transport. About halfway along the way to South Hill, the driver, Mr. McClain, spoke over his shoulder to Hancock.

"We're coming up on Big Fork, Alan. You may want to call it in."

"All right," responded Alan, reaching for the microphone. "Boydton resque 13 to South Hill ER on 3-4-0."

"This is South Hill. Go ahead, Boydton," the radio responded.

"South Hill, we have an eighty-two-year-old female complaining of dyspnea. She has a history of heart failure and hypertension. Her initial O2 sats were 90 percent on room air and she is comfortable on 2 liters of O2 with a sat of ..." He glanced at the oximeter to report the current reading. The screen of red digits began flashing mysteriously. All the numbers were sixes—oxygen saturation 66 percent and heart rate 666. "Ah... just a second," he stalled, checking the patient's finger probe sensor and the monitor leads. They were all in order. "Well, I'm not getting a reading now, but it was, ah... 99 percent with a pulse of 86, BP 138/72. ETA of six to eight minutes."

"We copy you, Boydton. Notify us of any changes. South Hill clear," was the response.

"Buddy," Alan said to the driver. "Has anyone reported the monitor malfunctioning?"

"Not that I've heard of."

"The displays went crazy! All sixes and flashing."

"Well, it does flash all eights for a few seconds when you cut it on. Do you think the power connection was shorted out somehow?"

"I don't know. Maybe." He rechecked their patient to assure stability. Despite what the electronics had indicated, she was in no distress. By the time of their arrival to the ER, the digital readings displayed a mundane 98 percent saturation and a heart rate of 82.

The day following this bizarre call, a familiar form appeared in Dr. Hardy's office, leaning in on the registration counter. It was near the end of office hours so Dr. Hardy was relieved it wasn't an additional patient seeking care, only Alan Hancock from Boydton Life Station. Alan recounted the night's call and the deranged monitor episode.

"I just don't know," he stated. "The monitor was new with Unit 13."

"Unit 13?" said Lucy. "That's unlucky!"

"Yeah. We went over that at our squad meeting," he said wryly. "But I've checked the monitor three times since. It works perfectly."

"Strange," said Dr. Hardy. "Could you switch monitors with another ambulance just to see?"

"Yeah. I guess so. We can try that." Although Alan was never at a loss for words, he paused before continuing. "When I cleaned the back after the call, there was a patch of blood on the floor. It looked familiar to me and I realized it was shaped like the splatter left when Greg Jackson coded en route."

"Maybe it was the stain left from then," suggested Lucy. Alan shook his head.

"Nope. This blood was still wet. A triangular-shaped smear with three drops around it."

"Well, maybe you just spilled some blood with this patient and it looked kind of similar," said Dr. Hardy.

"Nope. I started her IV clean, no drips. And I checked it when we unloaded her. It wasn't leaking."

"That's creepy!" said Lucy.

"Coincidence. It's just a coincidence!" Dr. Hardy said assuredly. "There's nothing weird about it!"

"Uh-huh," Hancock said with a skeptical air. "Well, I'll try switching out the monitors. I'll keep you posted."

"All right," replied Hardy.

M ark McClain was in Clarksville on the location of a "hot" new story. Freeman's Funeral Home had burned in a mysterious early-morning fire. The three-alarm fire had drawn fire crews from Boydton and Chase City to assist Clarksville. It was the first fire in the town limits for decades, and despite the efforts of the volunteer fire fighters, the building was largely reduced to ashes. Lingering spots still steamed with gray smoke vapor, creating an eerie fog. Some metal caskets appeared to have escaped major damage other than black scorching. Other coffins, wooden structures, showed more severe stages of incineration. McClain strained to see if any of the burned coffins seemed to be occupied. Fire investigator Bruce Duffer was walking among the black, muddy ashes. McClain was compelled to ask him.

"Were there any—"

"Bodies?" Duffer interrupted with a knowing smile. "No. Fortunately not!"

"Good," McClain replied, a bit relieved. Funeral homes were ordinarily spooky enough, but with scathed coffins, hot ashes, and a mist of smoke, this was downright frightening. "Any clues as to the cause?"

"Well, naturally, I first assumed a cremation furnace accident.

However, Mr. Freeman," Duffer said, addressing a black man standing nearby, "said he hadn't installed one yet. Right?"

"That's right," the man nodded. He was Walter Freeman, the director of Freeman's Funeral Home. Even in the face of this disaster, he wore his formal dress shirt and tie. He was in his late thirties and wore a neatly trimmed mustache.

"I've questioned the firemen and other witnesses. It seems the origin of the fire was the hearse," Duffer stated.

"Well, it was parked in back, under the carport," Freeman said.

"Yeah. The blaze lit the carport roof and spread up to the building's roof. It was a hot burn."

"When was your last funeral?" asked Mark.

"About three weeks ago," responded Freeman. "But we did deliver a coffin the week after that."

"Deliver a coffin?" Mark queried.

"Well, yeah. A lady found our coffins to be less expensive and requested that we deliver one to Walker Funeral Home for a relative of hers."

"That's odd, isn't it?"

"I guess, but Walker marks up his caskets 30 to 40 percent higher than ours. We use the same suppliers. She was only being practical."

"It makes good business sense, I reckon," Mark said. "Oh, I'm curious. Who was the decedent?"

"Ah ... a Jackson. Greg Jackson, I think."

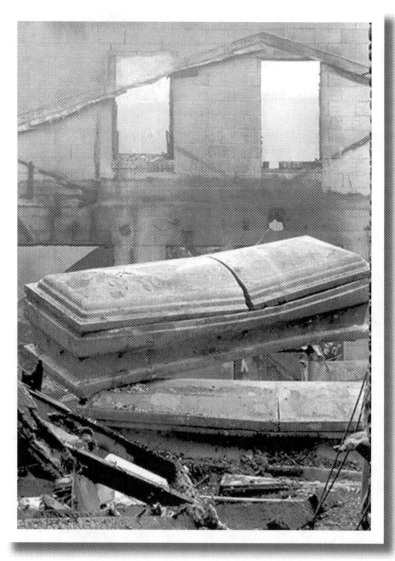

Photo courtesy of South Boston News & Record

Chapter 18

Further Studies

The Bluestone Senior High gymnasium in June was a bit stuffy and warm, despite the heat-pump cooling system, as a crowd amassed for the commencement ceremony. Dr. Hardy, Lucy, and Anna secured seats in the aluminum bleachers. This year's event was tainted bittersweet as there was an empty seat among the graduates. Jolanda White's cap was laid in her designated chair in a display of homage to an accomplished senior, but also a somber reminder of her fatal swim.

Vikki Hardy was an honor graduate and governor's school student, noted as well for her involvement in the debate team, robotics, the school band, and the Junior Women's Association. Her class size of 148 was reminiscent of Dr. Hardy's senior class here nearly forty years ago. Their speaker stressed the role of education, essential now for achieving prosperity in our high tech, computerized society.

After all the "circumstances" of addresses and awards, they finally advanced to the "pomp" of the diploma progression. Vikki stood in the line for the stage, her navy blue cap and gown accented with a shiny golden stole embroidered with "Honor." She appeared collected, for she hardly ever displayed nervousness. Lucy stood up and struggled to zoom in her camera on the diploma bestowal. Mark McClain had a sideline seat at stage front, gathering his photojournalism bits. When Lucy sat back down, Dr. Hardy patted her thigh. His eyes were watery as he spoke.

"We did something right," he said proudly.

"Yeah, we did," Lucy said with a beaming smile.

The energy from excited young people in the parking lot beside the gym emanated through the crowd. Congratulations, farewell hugs, high fives, and photos abounded. Dr. Hardy hugged Vikki and kissed her forehead.

"I'm so proud of you!" he said, for the third time.

"Thanks, Dad!" She then added, "Oh, can I go to the lake with my friends?"

Dr. Hardy felt a chill as Jolanda's death flashed back to him. He looked at Lucy. Vikki was an excellent swimmer and, now, a responsible high school graduate.

"I guess so," he said reluctantly. "Is that okay?" he asked his wife.

"Yeah," she said. "But be home for supper!"

"Okay! Thanks!" Vikki said, turning to leave. She abruptly came back and added, "Can Anna go with us?" She smiled eagerly at Anna. Her sister had been like a fifth wheel throughout the day. To be asked to share in Vikki's celebration was a heartwarming endorsement. Vikki would be leaving their home soon, and this demonstrated she still planned to include her sister in her life.

"Sure, if she wants to go," smiled Lucy.

A grinning Anna took off with Vikki, calling back, "Bye, Mom! Bye, Dad!"

B uddy McClain drove Unit 13 on an evening EMS call to assist a patient with stomach pains and vomiting. The medical attendant in the back of the ambulance was Della. She was a little pudgy, short-statured, with dirty blond hair but a seasoned emergency care provider. Following her care protocols, she had started IV fluids and given odansetron for nausea. Her patient's condition was much improved as they traveled toward South Hill Hospital. Della was busy recording the medical history on her touch screen electronic notebook. As she was entering the vital signs, she looked up at the monitor display for the most current readings. Suddenly, the overhead light flickered and the screen display lit up in green sixes—heart rate 666 and oxygen saturation 66 percent. Della frantically glanced at the patient and, then all around her. She promptly climbed up into the front cab and sat down on the passenger's seat. Buddy studied her actions inquisitively, noting she was wide eyed, pale, and tremulous.

"What's up?"

"The monitor!" she gasped. "It just went crazy! All sixes!"

"No kidding? That happened with Alan, too!"

"Yeah. I heard about that."

"It's kinda creepy!"

"And not only that, the air turned cool and damp. It felt like a fog or something." She added softly, "I'm telling you, this ambulance is haunted!" Her tone was dead serious. They rode in silence for two minutes.

"You know, you gotta get back there," stated Buddy.

"Yeah," Della responded. "I know." She hesitantly crawled back into the rear.

At the end of the run, Buddy backed Unit 13 into the squad's base garage. The attendant in charge, or AIC, usually performed the disinfecting of the patient care area. Della was slow to get up from her front seat.

"I'll clean the back if you close the bay door and hook up the charger," offered Buddy.

"Okay, deal!" responded Della, eagerly.

Buddy was sweeping the ambulance floor when he found a soiling of blood. It was in a triangular shape with three spatters of blood around it. He froze momentarily before he wiped away the still wet stain.

Robert Meadows presented for his appointment with Dr. Hardy. Hardy read his vital signs from his chart.

"Three pounds," he said, shaking his head. "It is better, but not even a 2 percent weight loss."

"Well, Doc," Meadows said, "I've changed my eating habits for the better."

"All right. We'll get some labs to check how much you've improved."

"Okay. Oh, by the way, we found out some more about that old skull we found."

"Oh, yeah?"

"Yeah. It appears that it is of Native American origin."

"I guess they couldn't tell how he died, could they?"

"Nope, but he probably died between 1850 and 1900."

"Thanks. I'll tell Vikki about it. She's planning to go to JMU this fall."

"All right. That's good," he said, rolling up his shirt sleeve. "Send in your vampire."

The following week, the central office's ME report on Greg Jackson came in. Dr. Hardy reviewed the findings with Lucy and Loren during their office lunch break.

"Cause of death: seizures, due to alcohol withdrawal. Manner of death: natural," he read.

"Alcohol withdrawal? While in jail?" asked Lucy.

"Well, he was on the work release program and, apparently, got wasted at the wine festival."

"Yeah, but he's been drunk many a time. Why do you think this killed him?" she asked.

"Since he was incarcerated, he'd been dry. His body wasn't exposed to everyday drinking. So, his usual amount of alcohol was then more toxic to him. When he returned to jail, he went cold turkey. He couldn't block the DTs with more alcohol. Also, he had some organ damage from his substance abuse. It reads *Cardiomyopathy, nonischemic,* which can come from chemical damage, usually alcohol, drugs, or diabetes."

"Sounds like he dug his own grave," said Loren.

"Yeah. And his toxicologies were positive for cocaine and THC—marijuana. We call it 'holiday heart.' It couldn't tolerate the stresses of withdrawal—elevated heart rate and blood pressure."

"So," said Lucy, "what happens to our escrow money now?"

"I guess we deal with his estate or lawyer."

"If he was going to die anyway, why didn't he just do it before he filed this suit against us?"

"I'm sure he didn't plan his death to inconvenience us, even if he could have."

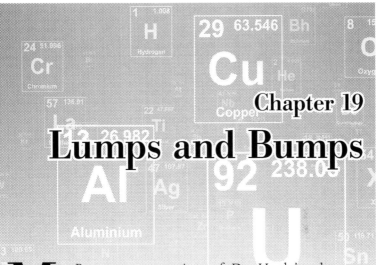

Chapter 19

Lumps and Bumps

Mr. Bracey was a patient of Dr. Hardy's who was undergoing an excision of three skin lesions. He suffered from neurofibromatosis, leaving his skin riddled with hundreds of fleshy nodules ranging from the size of a raisin to a large grape. In the past, Dr. Hardy had sent off a few for pathologic analysis, all showing only benign fibromas.

"You been to any medical examiner cases recently?" asked Bracey, while under the knife.

"Not really," he answered.

"I saw you at the Clarksville Bridge when that man fell back in the fall."

"Oh, yeah? You were there?"

"Yep. I listen to the scanners and go see stuff that's happening."

An ambulance chaser, thought Hardy as he tied off his suture. "I guess that's interesting."

"Yeah."

Dr. Hardy removed his paper field drape, revealing his stitches nestled in a field of budding neurofibromas covering Mr. Bracey's front torso.

"You know," said Hardy, "I've taken a dozen of these things off of you over the past two years. I can't see any difference in your skin."

"Yeah, but it is better. We'll keep picking at them. See you in three months?" he said.

"Yeah. I guess so. Have Lucy take out those stitches—"

"In seven to ten days," said Bracey, experienced with the routine. He smiled as he stood to leave. "Thanks, Doc!"

It was Wednesday afternoon, which meant Dr. Hardy might have time to go for a run and have a beer before supper. The sunny July afternoon had reached a humid ninety degrees but did not stifle Dr. Hardy's favorite exercise routine. By the time he reached the end of his half-mile driveway, his T-shirt was soaked in perspiration. He peeled off the shirt and hung it over a road sign post as he turned down the paved roadway. His dog enjoyed running with him, usually trotting out ahead, scouting the ditches and roadside woods. Today, he followed behind Dr. Hardy, his tongue hanging low, panting in the heat. By the end of the two-mile run, Hardy had become giddy and longed for a plunge in the lake. He paused, sitting on the shaded porch, to gather his strength for walking the trail to the water.

"Obie," Lucy called to him. "The 9-1-1 operator called for you. There's an ME case."

Mr. Bracey's question jinxed me, he thought. "All right," he responded weakly, realizing the swim and a beer would have to wait.

Despite a quick shower, Dr. Hardy continued to sweat during his commute. The call had summoned him to the North Carolina side of the lake again, south of Clarksville. The evening was still sultry, even as the sun was setting behind the Clarksville skyline. He turned onto State Line Road to reach Old Soudan Road. Despite living around Buggs Island Lake most of his life, Dr. Hardy had never visited this recreational area, Old Soudan Park. It was just four miles off Route 15. Dusk was falling when he parked in the graveled area beside the county cruisers. A deputy greeted him.

"Dr. Hardy?"

"Yeah."

"You can follow me back to the scene," he said, turning toward the woods. "That's the decedent's car there." He pointed at a light gray Oldsmobile that was backed into place beside the entrance of a path. Hardy noted a tennis shoe on the ground beside the driver's door. The deputy had started down the walkway. It was paved, an unusually nice trail for such an isolated site. "This is the old road bed," the deputy explained. "The bridge across Grassy Creek to Merrifield used to come off this point before the lake was built."

"Oh, yeah? I never knew that."

"Supposedly, it's a good fishing site."

As they proceeded beneath the trees, it had become darker. Dr. Hardy appreciated that the deputy carried two large flashlights. The officer had on one and shined it along the pavement, which was littered with leaves and twigs.

Snake camouflage, Dr. Hardy thought of the forest debris. These cold-blooded reptiles would be active on such a hot night and probably drawn to the heat retained by the pavement as the air cooled.

"Careful," said the deputy. "Here's where we get off the road."

Off the road? thought Hardy, a little concerned. The deputy aimed the light off their solid trail into the bushes where several predecessors had trod a crude footpath. After picking their way through the brush, Dr. Hardy could see the flickering of flashlights up ahead. The scene was about 150 yards from the parking area.

Detective Duffer was on the bank and Carl Wilborn was knee-deep in the lake water. Duffer cast his light at Wilborn's feet.

"Here's the decedent, presumably thirty-seven-year-old Lamont Stillman. He was found here, near the bank, floating facedown," Duffer reported. Small insects danced in his light's beam.

"How did anyone find him back here?" inquired Dr. Hardy.

"Fishermen found him about 5:45 p.m.," explained Duffer. "He left Oxford about 4 a.m., according to his sister there. Supposedly, he was on his way to Petersburg." He slapped the side of his neck. "Damned mosquitoes!"

Dr. Hardy laid his thermometer in the water, anchoring it with a stone. He looked at the dimly lit corpse floating just below the water's surface, face down. Lamont Stillman was an overweight, young adult black male wearing a gray tank top shirt and jean shorts. Oddly, he wore only his left sock and no shoes. His feet pointed ashore as he bobbed, submerged in the knee-deep water. Detective Wilborn stood in the shallows at his head, blocking him from drifting aweigh. Dr. Hardy was at the water's edge, straining to focus amid the water's distortion and the harsh flashlight illumination.

"Can we roll him over?" asked Hardy.

"Sure, Doc," replied Wilborn. He reached down and rotated the shoulders of the body, exposing his face. No signs of injury were apparent except for a postmortem nasal abrasion from the lake bottom. Curiously, his shorts were unzipped.

"Maybe he was urinating on the bank," proposed Dr. Hardy.

"Or dressing hastily," added Duffer. He flashed several photos as he was speaking. "His wallet was left on the car seat, as if he planned to get wet or take off his shorts. There was one shoe bedside the car, and we found the other one on the beach about twenty yards from here, with the other sock."

"Strange," noted Hardy. "Can we pull him out of the water?"

"Yeah, sure," said Wilborn. Holding the body by the armpits, he floated it to the shore and slid him onto the body bag that Duffer had spread out. Hardy read the water temperature, eighty-two degrees, and moved the thermometer to the decedent's armpit. He pulled out a pen and began making notes on his clipboard.

"Okay, Bruce, do you have a birth date?" he asked. It was a moonless night, and he strained to see the paper in the pitch dark. The guide deputy provided some writing light for Hardy.

"Yes, it's 4-11-73," said Duffer. A swarm of gnats, moths, and mosquitoes circled in the flashlight beam. Hardy felt the bugs striking his face and eyes as he recorded the date. Some gnats were sticking to the sweat on his forehead.

"Last seen alive?" he asked, squinting and blinking to protect his eyes.

"4 a.m. in Oxford," reported Duffer.

"Cut off the light and let the bugs scatter!" Hardy suggested.

"Okay," said the deputy.

"Do you have an address?"

"Yes. 269 Alexander Drive, Petersburg," said Duffer. With the loss of the bright light, Dr. Hardy was as blind as ever.

"Light," he said. A battalion of winged pests appeared within the bright column. They invaded Hardy's nose and mouth. "Ptth!" This was a futile endeavor. "Can we do this in the car?"

"Sure," Duffer agreed.

Hardy collected his axillary temperature, eighty-six degrees. This indicated the time of death was at least eight to ten hours earlier. Retreating to the parking area, Hardy sat in Duffer's Crown Victoria cruiser and recorded his details.

"I'll call this into Richmond. He'll need an autopsy," Dr. Hardy concluded.

"Good luck. I couldn't get a cell signal here," said Duffer.

"Great! Seems like if anyone dies mysteriously in Mecklenburg County, it's in a dead zone! I'll call it in from home and fax my CME-1."

"Okay. Freeman's Funeral Home is en route."

Back home, Hardy phoned the Richmond ME office as he completed his report form.

"Did you get anything to eat?" Lucy asked. "We did a pizza and salad."

"I did have a snack," he said, recalling the bugs in his mouth. "Pizza would great." He added, "And a beer that I've been craving."

"I'll get you one," she said, smiling.

It was nearly midnight when they got to bed. The drawn-out croaks of the tree frogs were the only sounds. Suddenly, there were three bangs from upstairs.

"Did you hear that?" exclaimed Lucy.

"Yeah!"

"It sounded like hammering!"

"Yes, it did!" Before they could speak again, another sound arose. *Clomp, clomp, clomp, clomp.*

"Somebody's walking around up there!" Lucy said. "Do you think it's Greg? His ghost?"

Obie Hardy remembered the bizarre happenings Alan had experienced in Unit 13. That had been on the same night he had heard the noise in his house. A chill spread over his body.

"I'll go check it out," he said, resigning himself to action. At the top of the stairs, he first looked in his daughters' bedrooms. Both were sleeping soundly. He then proceeded to the unfinished bonus room over his bedroom. Strangely, a light shone from under the door. He opened the door and found the room well lit but eerily empty. After surveying the space to assure vacancy, he turned off the light and closed the door. There had to be a logical explanation for this phenomenon, but right now a spiritual possession seemed most likely.

Dr. Hardy and Lucy had a restless night, and when he got ready for morning hospital rounds at five forty-five, he found Anna asleep on the den sofa.

"Are you okay?" he asked, touching her shoulder.

"Yeah. I woke up and it just felt creepy, so I came down here."

Hardy kissed her on the forehead. "It's okay," he said, but was uncertain that it was.

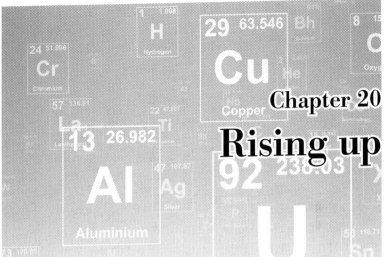

Chapter 20

Rising up

Dr. Hardy was completing his weekly nursing home visits at Meadowview Terrace. Harrison Woods, the cerebral palsy patient usually plagued with repulsive odors, was neat, well groomed, and fresh smelling. He was cheerful, smiling, and obviously benefitted from the staff's added hygienic care. Garland Gear reported to Dr. Hardy that his bowels were functioning regularly and his abdomen remained pain-free. Dr. Hardy felt pride, pleased the care he had directed for his patients was so effective. Then, on the drive home, he remembered Julie Newby and her witchcraft spells.

Nah, he thought, *it couldn't be from that!* He couldn't, however, dispel that notion. He hadn't really done anything different.

At home, Lucy met him, fanning her face with her hand.

"It's eighty-five degrees upstairs now!" she exclaimed. "The heat pump's tore up!"

"What? That unit only draws eight gallons a minute from the well when it's running constantly. We should have enough water flow for it!"

"Well, it's not working! I've called Bluestone Heating and Air. They haven't called back yet."

"Okay." It was August, the peak of summer heat. He had anticipated converting the upstairs geothermal unit to a closed loop, underground system when they settled the escrow. Now, his hand was called. "We'll need to convert it to the closed system now."

"I hope it won't take long! Vikki and Anna can't sleep upstairs in this heat!" Dr. Hardy thought the heat wasn't the only thing sending Anna downstairs to the den couch.

"We'll get it done," he assured her.

It was a little over a week before Bluestone Heating and Air could arrange to do the conversion. Lucy had recruited her brother, Butch, to run the backhoe they had leased for the project. Butch had driven up from Florida to help his little sister. The piping system required parallel trenches spanning the lengths of more than two football fields. Butch worked tirelessly, creating the ditches that spread over most of the front yard, doubling back alongside one another. On the second day, in the far corner of the yard, he encountered some construction debris just below the ground surface.

Lucy made lunch at the house for Dr. Hardy and Butch, giving the Hardys an opportunity to check on the progress.

"You won't believe what I found out there," said Butch. "A pile of construction trash!"

"Oh, yeah," Dr. Hardy responded. "Greg had asked if he could make a burn pile out there somewhere."

"Well, he put it in your front yard, and it's mostly full of beer cans!"

"Beer cans?" said Lucy.

"Yep. Hundreds, I'm sure," Butch said, raising his eyebrows. "You want to see them?"

Dr. Hardy and Lucy looked at each other and replied in unison, "Yes."

The barren, red-clay residential lot was now marred by long furrows. They made their way to the garbage dump that Butch had unearthed. There were fragments of bricks, charred wood, and strips of metal lying in a nest of empty beer cans. Some cans had black scorching on them, but most looked like everyday roadside litter.

"Jackson's Bar and Grill," stated Dr. Hardy.

"Yeah," replied Butch. "Probably not the best work environment."

"Well, that explains some things," said Lucy.

"Yeah, but nothing we hadn't expected," Dr. Hardy responded, picking up a sample can from the pile.

Back inside, he placed the buried-treasure souvenir on the kitchen island. "This might prove useful in settling the escrow."

Just then, the can began quivering curiously. The house commenced to tremble and a low-pitched rumbling sound like faraway thunder arose.

"Wow!" said Dr. Hardy. "You can really feel him digging with that backhoe!"

Then, from behind Dr. Hardy, Butch spoke. "What backhoe?" Hardy suddenly realized this was not from heavy equipment vibrations. "That's an earthquake!" exclaimed Butch.

Everything settled to a quiet stillness.

"An earthquake? In Virginia?" asked Lucy.

"Well, we had one here a few years ago," said Hardy. They all peered at the bent beer can, and Dr. Hardy felt a cool sensation flow up his spine.

Clomp-clomp-clomp-clomp. They heard the sound of boots walking on the floor upstairs.

"You hear that?" exclaimed Lucy. "Like someone's walking up there!"

Butch, looking up with eyebrows raised, spoke again. "It's probably just some settling of the house, from the earthquake." His analysis, however practical, convinced none of them.

Mark McClain stood outside of the unfinished BLS building, focusing his camera on the partially bricked wall. There was a crooked, step-shaped crack down the masonry work. He was astonished that a record-breaking earthquake with an epicenter in Virginia and felt as far away as New York would cause so little damage to Mecklenburg County. Other than some residences with plaster cracks to their inside walls, there was no newsworthy destruction. The earthquake had registered 5.9 on the Richter scale, surpassing the previous most powerful one in Virginia in 1897. There had been a quake a couple of years ago of a 3.6 severity. As Mark studied a list of these events on his computer, he wondered if the Virginia earthquake frequency was increasing. This was the third one since 2003. He decided to ask a scientist.

"Well," began James Callahan, the SVCC earth science professor, "this is our strongest yet, and the third one in ten years. Since 1800 we have had about seven earthquakes a century. It's too soon to conclude that they're more frequent. They may just be clustered in the first half of this century."

"Good," said Mark.

"Virginia is not on a geologic fault like California. The earth's mantle sits on a configuration of slabs called tectonic plates. The Pacific Plate and the North American Plate join under California, the San Andreas Fault line. The other edge of the North American Plate runs under the mid-Atlantic Ocean. We're not at risk for our state splitting in two."

"Well, James, I'm surprised that there was so little damage."

"There was some *invisible* damage. The cell phone system crashed for hours after the quake due to an overload of calls."

"Yeah! Mine was out then too. Thanks for the info."

"Oh! We're on for the kyanite mine tour next month! I'll keep you posted."

"Great! And thanks!" He now had enough data to write an interesting article about this seismic phenomenon.

I t was the evening before Vikki Hardy was scheduled to move to her James Madison University dormitory. The Hardys were loading the Jeep and Vikki's black Cavalier for the trek. Gathering some books and accessories from Vikki's room, Dr. Hardy noticed the tarot card deck.

"Oh, that's Anna's," said Vikki, removing the deck from her lot. "She had them in my room doing a reading. She's teaching me some of the art."

"Okay," said Obie Hardy. Then, an idea struck him. "Anna," he called.

"What?" she responded.

"Could you do a tarot reading tonight in the bonus room?"

"Why? You still think it's haunted?"

"Well... I don't know. Would a reading tell us if it is?"

"I couldn't say. I'll do one there if you'd like to," she offered.

"Great!"

They finished loading the vehicles and had supper. Vikki kept a suitcase open in her room for her overnight toiletries and last-minute additions.

"When do you want to do the reading?" asked Anna.

"I was thinking around eleven thirty or twelve. We have usually heard the noises around midnight," said Obie Hardy.

When the late-night news came on TV, Hardy called everyone to assemble in the bonus room. Anna laid down a large Harley-Davidson beach towel with a giant skull in the center. She lit three black candles and sat at one end of the towel.

"You guys can sit at that end," she directed.

"Where'd you get the black candles?" asked Lucy.

"Spencer's," she answered.

"Do you want the light on or off?" asked Obie Hardy.

"Off," she said. "We'll use just the candles."

"And this," said Obie, placing the excavated beer can in front of Anna. "This is from the beer cans he buried in our front yard."

"Okay. Great," she said. "To ask about spirits and departed souls, the Ouija board is a better tool than tarot cards." She placed the black-lettered, brown board in front of her. "Vikki can sit across from me and we'll both touch the reader. Now, everyone must focus only on the questions, deep concentration. We must channel our psychic energies. Any skepticism or humor will disrupt the connection."

She nodded to Vikki, and they placed their fingertips lightly along the edges of the teardrop-shaped glider. "Greg Jackson, are you still among us in spirit?" she chanted.

The room was eerily silent for about a minute before the indicator slowly inched to the left corner of the board before stopping over the *yes*. The sisters' eyes met, and Dr. Hardy looked at Lucy, the dim candle flames shedding a haunting light on their silhouettes.

Anna rubbed the Ouija indicator in circles across the board, as if erasing the message.

"Okay," she stated, reaching out again to position her fingers along the indicator. Vikki mirrored her action. "Why do you still linger here?" she inquired in her monotone.

After a breathless pause, the reader began creeping over the alphabet letters, stalling over the letter *D*. With their psychic energies focused, they heard, in the soundless room, the soft, streaking sound of the Ouija reader as it moved around the board. The subsequent letters revealed were *E, P, O, G, O, N,* and *E*. After these, there were only a few random twitches, and no new letters emerged.

Dr. Hardy felt as if they were being watched. Another presence permeated the room. The candle flames flickered, as if in a breeze, then went out. The darkness was only momentary, however, as the overhead lightbulb in the bonus room came on. The Hardys gazed at one another in silence. Suddenly, Vikki stood up, breaking the intensity.

"Well, I'm going to JMU in the morning!" she exclaimed anxiously.

"Can I go with you?" Lucy pleaded.

Probing

The second week of school, James Callahan's earth science class set out on a field trip to the nearby kyanite mine. Anna Hardy had been selected for the governor's school program and was enrolled in Callahan's class.

Mark McClain, to avoid getting up so early, had spent the night in Farmville with Vanessa. Saving sleep, although, hardly mattered, since they spent more time awake in bed than asleep. Vanessa drove her car to capture the work-related mileage.

"So, what are we looking for?" she asked.

"I don't know," Mark answered truthfully. "A tall black man like the motel clerk described, alkaline chemicals, suspicious behavior."

"I see." She paused briefly. "Basically, a wild goose chase, huh?"

"Yep. Or more like a snipe hunt." He alluded to the old forest prank, which left the victim alone, awaiting the fictitious prey.

"You got your snipe sack?"

"Yeah." He held up his digital camera, smiling.

They followed the SVCC activities bus to Willis Mountain, continuing up Willis Mountain Plant Road to the mine site. At the administrative building, Vanessa and Mark joined the thirty-eight students in the meeting room. A middle-aged lady with sandy-colored hair addressed the assembly.

"I'd like to welcome Professor Callahan and all of you on your tour of our mining operation. I'm Eva Layton, chief of marketing here at American Kyanite. I'll give you a quick overview of the company." Mark snapped some pictures as she continued.

"The mining site on Willis Mountain was pioneered by the first geology graduate of Virginia Tech. Unfortunately, his venture went bankrupt in the 1940s. Currently, this is the largest kyanite mine in the world, capable of producing 150,000 tons of kyanite annually. Kyanite is a mineral used in porcelain, spark plug insulation, automotive brake shoes, and in high-temperature kilns and furnaces. A few gemologists even set kyanite stones in jewelry."

After some informal questions and answers, they were prepared to view the mining. "We usually tour smaller groups so you will shuttle off, taking turns, in groups of eight."

Their tour buses were a pair of four-wheeled ATVs, each able to accommodate a driver and four passengers, if the leanest three shared the back bench seat. A group of students donned hard hats and rolled off in the first of five waves.

"The second mule driver is black," Mark said softly to Vanessa. "Be sure you ride with him, and I'll take a photo to show to the motel clerk."

"All right," she responded. "But, she described him as tall and slender. That driver was pretty short and stout."

"Yeah, I know. But I'm grabbing at straws."

As he photographed Vanessa, he smiled, seeing her in a hard hat, riding shotgun in a mining vehicle.

Since he was not officially a part of the school group, when Vanessa rode off, he took the opportunity to wander about the complex. He photographed the few workers he encountered, none seeming to match the suspect's physique. The only crime apparent here was the scathing of the mountain, the processed stone chunks being reduced to large fields of rocky mine tailings. A protocol geared at rebuilding the mountain and reforestation was not apparent. This could have been the violation Phil Bentley had discovered. When he returned to the administrative building, he asked Ms. Layton about this.

"Well, it's not as simple as you would think. It's not like piling up the tailings back on the mountain top. The stone is loose and unstable. It doesn't support root growth well and is subject to accelerated erosion. The run-off contaminates the land and streams with silt. The tailing fields are an intermediary phase but are more resistant to erosion."

"Okay. I can see that," Mark said. *Maybe there are significant environmental issues that Bentley discovered*, he thought. "Oh, is there any way I can buy a kyanite ore sample?"

"Sure," she said. "I'll give you some rough chips I have in my office ... and a sample for Callahan's classroom too."

"Great! Thanks!"

As the college bus pulled out from the mine site, Mark and Vanessa headed back to the Country Court Lodge in nearby Sprouses Corner. Fortunately, the motel clerk, Shirley, was on duty. Mark showed her the digital photos of mining personnel.

"No," she said. "I'm sorry. It wasn't any of those men who checked in."

"You're sure?" pressed Mark.

"Positive."

"All right. Thanks again!"

D r. Hardy and Lucy were leaving Boydton to pick up Anna from the field trip. It was a Saturday afternoon, and since they would be in Keysville already, Lucy had planned for them to continue to the Colonial Heights shopping plazas afterward.

"You know, Lucy," Dr. Hardy said, "I'm not sure about the Ouija board message, *depo gone*. At first, with the beer can there, I thought, *the beer can depot is gone now*."

"Yeah, that makes sense," said Lucy.

"Then, I remembered, we had *depo*sitions scheduled. They're unfinished business now, and *gone*."

"Maybe so."

Dr. Hardy's phone buzzed. "Hello. Dr. Hardy here."

"This is the medical examiner's office, Dr. Hardy. Could you do a viewing and draw blood on a case?"

"Ah ... how urgent is it? I'm on the way out of town."

"That's okay. We just need it within the next twelve hours. It is a hanging."

"Where's the body?" he asked.

"Draper's Funeral Home in South Hill."

"Okay, but it might be seven or eight o'clock before I could be there."

"That's fine. We've already got the information for the CME-1 form."

"All right. I'll do it this evening."

"An ME case?" asked Lucy.

"Yeah. It's in South Hill. We can come home that way and I'll do it."

The activities bus arrived at the John Daniels Campus of SVCC just ahead of the Hardy's. The county school buses were on-site to carry students home who weren't being met.

"Professor Callahan," Dr. Hardy called out. He had brought his state geological map with him to share with James Callahan.

"Yes?" he responded, recognizing the doctor. "Dr. Hardy."

"A geologist gave me a geologic map. I thought you might like to see it." He held up the map, rolled into a long tube.

"Oh, yeah?" Callahan responded curiously. "I'd like that. Come inside to the classroom, if you will."

They unrolled the map on Callahan's desk, with Lucy and Anna looking on.

"The geologist is one of my patients. He was assuring me that there was no gold on my farm."

Callahan chuckled. "This is fascinating!" he exclaimed. "Would you allow me to borrow this for a while? For my classes? I'll get a plastic cover to protect it."

"Sure. That would put it to good use," Dr. Hardy said, agreeing.

When the Hardys finally headed home, they traveled Interstate 85 into South Hill. Dusk was approaching, but the August evening was still stifling hot. Dr. Hardy parked in the shaded, covered side entrance of Draper's Funeral Home.

"If you guys just wait here, I'll be just twenty minutes or so. You can roll the windows down if you like." He stepped outside and noted the heady odor of a dead animal. He glanced along the roadside searching for a possible roadkill source. When he turned back toward the funeral home, a reality struck him. *Is that smell from the body I'm here to see?* he thought.

"What's that smell?" asked Lucy, through her open window. "It smells like something died."

"Yeah," he replied, walking off toward the back entrance. At the back door, he was greeted by the assistant funeral director.

"Good evening, Dr. Hardy. I'm glad to see you."

"I can imagine," Hardy replied. The odor grew more pungent as the door was opened. "Is this smell from him?"

"I'm afraid so. It is summer, you know. We've had the exhaust fan running all day." They walked into the prep room.

"It's not air-conditioned back here?" Hardy asked incredulously.

"Nope. Just out in the chapel area. Here's the body, Marvin Porterman." He indicated the decomposing human form lying on the steel table. The thick stench filling the room was smothering. Dr. Hardy ascertained that the body was tainted by an advanced level of decay. The head was black and swollen, the bulging eyelids tightly closed. Dark, coffee-like purge liquid oozed from the plump lips. A heavily braided nylon ligature remained tied around the neck. Hardy estimated his height to be five foot nine and weight about 170 pounds. His race was indeterminable from his face, but his arms and torso appeared Caucasian. The thin, outer skin layer had begun to shed like that of an onion, the smell of which would have been an improvement. The extremities exhibited full rigor mortis, even involving the jaw.

"He must have been dead for over twelve hours," Hardy stated.

"Yeah. They found him about nine last night. He'd probably been dead at least eight hours then."

Hardy slid the jeans down enough to expose the inguinal folds and made repetitive passes with the needle seeking a blood sample. Including similar stabs in the opposite groin, his efforts yielded only a few cc of black, watery fluid.

The eyelids were boggy and swollen firmly shut, forcing Hardy to make a blind stick through the soft tissue, into the side of the globe. He was rewarded with 2 cc of clear, watery, vitreous fluid. After tapping the second eye, his completed harvest was two tubes of liquids, one clear and one cola-colored.

Dr. Hardy, longing for fresh air, returned to the Jeep to find the engine running. Lucy and Anna were in the front seats, their shirts pulled up over their noses like veiled Middle-Eastern women, the air conditioner blowing. He opened the back door.

"Dad, you ride back there!" Anna ordered.

"Yeah. This is gross!" said Lucy. "How can they let a body just lay out in this heat?"

"I guess AC is for the living," he replied. "Hey, how about we stop for some milkshakes?" He was hoping a treat might make up for their suffering. His question was met with icy stares across shirt collars.

Chapter 22

Thin Air

Anna came to Dr. Hardy's office after school. She worked on her homework at one of the computer desks. When Dr. Hardy completed his patient visits for the day, she spoke up.

"Dad! We got our radon test kits today for our science class project!"

"Didn't Vikki test our house last year?" he said.

"Yeah. We're doing a follow-up sampling. But we've got a new house to test this year, too!"

"Hmm, that's right," he said.

"You need to get ready for dance class," Lucy said to Anna.

"That's tonight?" asked Dr. Hardy.

"Yep," said Lucy.

"Well, I can go to the nursing home while y'all are at dance," he suggested.

"Okay, sure," said Lucy. "I'll bring home something for our dinner."

On Water Lily Lane at Meadowview, Dr. Hardy sat writing in the chart room. He was signing the monthly orders on Catherine High. She was chronically confused from Alzheimer's disease, but always pleasant and cheerful. Although she had the capability to walk, she preferred scooting herself about in a wheelchair. Dr. Hardy smiled as he wrote his exam note, recalling the six packages of cookies he had discovered hoarded under her blouse.

As he stepped out into the hall, he noticed a slim, blond nurse by the medicine cart. She wore a dark blue scrub top with silver stars and moons. It was Julie Newby, the good witch of the ward.

"Hi, Julie," he said as he approached.

"Hi, Dr. Hardy."

"I'm just curious, but … do you know anything about ghosts? Do you think they exist?"

"Absolutely! The spirits, or souls, of people can linger in our world. Usually trapped by an unresolved conflict."

"How long do they stay?"

"Indefinitely. They are not confined to our three dimensions. Time, the fourth dimension, is no boundary to spirits. They can move about, unlimited by clocks or calendars."

"Well…" Hardy hesitated and then said, "Suppose there was this ghost, or spirit. Is there something that can be done to get rid of it?"

"I suppose that, if their conflict could be resolved, the restless soul could move on to its afterlife destination."

"You mean, like heaven or hell?"

"Well, those are just labels. They are not locations or places that we can conceptualize. We can't imagine where they go."

"I see." Dr. Hardy pondered revealing to her his belief that he was being haunted. Maybe he could just tell her about the ambulance. "There was a patient who died in the ambulance en route to the hospital. Several rescue squad members have reported mysterious events occurring in the same ambulance—monitors malfunctioning, bloodstains. The dead patient happened to be the contractor who defaulted on their new building."

"Oh! That would be a major conflict! That is probably a real haunting," she said quite seriously.

"Wow," said Hardy. It took a few moments for him to muster the nerve to ask what he had originally pondered. "Do you feel that you could do a spell or something to get rid of this ghost?"

"An exorcism? Hmm, I don't know. I've never done one, but I have seen some incantations others have used."

"Could we hire you to give it a try?"

"I couldn't charge anything for it 'cause I don't know if it would help. It would be something I'd love to try. Would the rescue squad want me to do it?" Her eyes were sparkling with enthusiasm. She not only believed his plight was real, she was offering a solution. *Maybe*, he thought, *if she is successful with the ambulance, I might get her to exorcise my house.*

"Sure! Anytime you can arrange for it. They're on call 24-7."

"Great! I'll do some research and preparation and get back to you."

"You have no idea how much help this will be! Thanks, Julie."

After his encounter with Julie, Dr. Hardy was actually anxious to see Alan Hancock. True to form, it wasn't long before Alan made an habitual end-of-business-day visit to the office.

"Hancock, don't you ever work?" Hardy teased.

"It's quitting time, Doc."

"Yep. So what's happening with the rescue squad?"

"We have to file a suit against the contractor's estate to seek compensation for our losses."

"That'll be a hassle!"

"Yeah. He's gone and so is our money!" Alan appeared depressed. Hardy sensed that this might be a good time to address "fixing" the possessed ambulance.

"So, have there been any further haunting incidents in Unit 13?"

"Well, we haven't used it anymore." He sounded sad. "We save it as a back-up in case an ambulance breaks down or we have multiple calls at once."

"Okay. I'm not saying there are ghosts or not or that you have one or not. But I talked with a girl that dabbles in the supernatural and witchcraft. She believes spirits can get trapped while passing from life to the afterlife. Anyway, she has agreed to consult on our... ah, the squad's...situation."

"Like, perform an exorcism?" asked Alan, his eyes twinkling with excitement.

"Yeah. Something like that."

"That would be awesome! How did you find her?"

"Well, she's actually a nurse who works at the nursing home."

"Okay. We can be ready whenever she is available!"

Later that week, Dr. Hardy performed his chart work, reviewing prescription requests from his patients. Bruce Duffer's hypertension medicine was up for refills and it spurred Hardy's recollection of the recent hanging case. It might be a good time to telephone him.

"Bruce, it's Dr. Hardy," he said.

"Yeah. What's up?" answered Duffer.

"I just refilled your prescription."

"Okay. Thanks."

"I was just wondering. Did you work that hanging case last week? Porterman?"

"Yeah, the suicide. Why?"

"Well, the central office requested blood samples, but by the time I got there, he had decomposed so much that the specimens might not be any good. They didn't keep the body cooled."

"Oh, no! That may be bad. But, I got to try out the new COF sampler."

"*Cough?* What do you mean?"

"C-O-F, concentrated odor forensics," explained Duffer. "It's an experimental tool to find trace clues in the air around a crime scene."

"Oh! Vapors! I've heard about that! You used it at the scene?"

"Yeah. This case was perfect for trying it out. Although it took two hours to collect the sample before we could work the scene."

"Further body decay then too. How long before you get your readings?"

"I don't know, since it's new technology. Maybe two weeks or so," Duffer said.

"I'm anxious to see this stuff work. It seemed so science fiction."

"Yeah. I know."

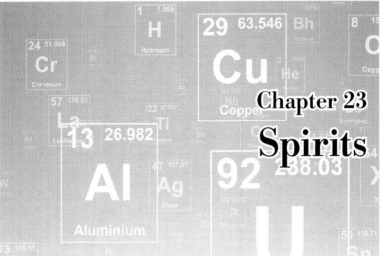

Chapter 23

Spirits

John Bancroft sat behind the antique oak desk in his law office meeting with Dr. Hardy and Lucy. He had been working on the escrow funds with Greg Jackson's estate attorney.

"You know your escrow balance is $89,000," began Bancroft. "Jackson's lawyer concedes that $30,000 was indeed your deposit and will be released to you. Apparently, he had spent the deposit, as these funds were not in his business account. That leaves $59,000 that is contested. Since the late Jackson is unable to support his claim now, they suggested a fifty-fifty split of the balance—$29,500 each."

"So, we'd get our thirty plus twenty-nine five?" asked Dr. Hardy.

"Yes. $59,500," stated Bancroft. "I thought it was a fair settlement, avoiding the expense of a court trial and judgment."

"I guess that's okay," said Lucy. She looked at Dr. Hardy with apparent acceptance. "What do you think?"

"Yeah. I'm okay with that," said Dr. Hardy. "I wish the rescue squad could get paid back for some of their damages, though."

"Well, that's another thing," Bancroft said. "The estate has proposed that their share of the escrow, $29,500, be paid to Boydton Life Station. Their defaulted claim was $32,816. They have agreed to accept this as a full settlement."

"That sounds even better," Lucy stated.

"Yes. I think that's a good proposal. Hardys 59, Rescue Squad 29, and Jackson Estate 0. A win-win!"

Another two weeks passed before Dr. Hardy received a report from Marvin Porterman's postmortem. Autopsy reports from the central office were routinely printed on yellow paper. This report, however, was on white paper with a blue header from Consolidated Labs, the forensics laboratory for the chief medical examiner of Virginia. It was his first Concentrated Odor Forensics, or COF, analysis.

The COF readings looked like a materials safety data sheet with a list of complex chemical compounds. Each item was tagged with one or more characters such as: *, °, †, or >. These notations were explained by a key on the second page. He found butyric acid, cadaverine, and putrescine each having asterisks with the key labeling the group as body decomposition aromas. This was quite understandable, since this body was not discovered promptly. Another pairing of highlighted chemical smells included PEG-8 distearate, PPG-14 butyl ether, and t-Beutylhydroquinone, components identified in these proportions in Brut deodorant.

Hmm, thought Hardy, *with these butyls, I can imagine how the name Brut arose.* Lastly, there was a cluster of isothiocyanates isolated. They were identified as byproducts of the breakdown of rhizome thioglucoside, more commonly known as wasabi.

"Wasabi?" he said aloud, hoping the sound of it would stimulate his recall.

"And hi ho, Silver, away!" Lucy responded. Absorbed in deciphering this new technology, Dr. Hardy had been unaware of her presence.

"No, not *kemosabe*! Wa-sabi."

"What's wasabi? It sounds familiar," she said.

"It's in this odor analysis from the scene of that hanging death," he explained.

"Oh! Wasabi. I think it's an Asian seasoning, maybe for seafood."

Although the eerie footsteps and lighting malfunctions did not occur daily, they still disturbed the Hardy home at least weekly. Since humans can adapt to repetitive noxious events and develop a tolerance, the Hardys were no longer gripped with fear by these now common occurrences. They felt more of an annoyance, as with an unwelcome guest. Nonetheless, Dr. Hardy was delighted when he received Julie's call about the ambulance exorcism.

"Dr. Hardy, I'm off this weekend if you want to set up our séance," she said cheerfully.

"All right! What night's best for you?" he asked eagerly.

"Probably Friday, October 1."

"Okay. I'll check with the rescue squad. I think we can just meet at the new rescue squad building site. What time?"

"Eight thirty to nine or so."

"Great. I'll see you then."

Lucy joined Dr. Hardy at the unfinished BLS building on Friday night. The October evening was mild, some patches of clouds jockeyed unsuccessfully to blot out the light of the rising moon. Dr. Hardy was relieved Julie hadn't chosen a midnight encounter for them. Buddy McClain and Alan drove the tainted Unit 13 into the garage bay area. Julie Newby promptly followed their arrival, carrying a dark cloth bag of accessories. Dr. Hardy introduced her to the others.

"This is Julie Newby. She practices the arts of nursing and witchcraft at Meadowview."

"Well, thanks. Although I rather prefer the Old English term of *wicca*," she said, smiling.

"Witchcraft, wicca, wizardry. I'll call it whatever you like if it gets rid of ghosts! Hi, I'm Alan, captain of Boydton Life Station. And this here is Buddy."

"Great. Now, do you think we could conduct this inside the ambulance?" she asked.

"Sure!" replied Alan. "We brought it just in case you wanted to."

"I'll need something like a small table to set up on," she said.

"I've got something," said Buddy, and he turned to leave.

"Good! And I'll need an offering of food or beverage to lure the spirit to us," Julie said as she carried the bag to the back of the ambulance.

"I know just the thing," Dr. Hardy stated. "I'll be back in a jiff." He left for the convenience store.

When Dr. Hardy returned, Julie had a toolbox cart placed between the bench seat and the patient cot in the ambulance. She had a scarf fitted over her head and tied in the back. It was divided down the center: one side a blue background with suns printed on it, the other side with moons on black. She wore a short navy cape with a satiny silver lining. There were three candles on her cart table. As she lit them, she explained their significance.

"The two white candles represent positive energy. The green one is for healing. I won't use my black candle since it is associated with negative energy." Hardy's eyes met Lucy's, recalling the black candles Anna had used at their home séance. "And the treat...," Julie said looking at Dr. Hardy, "goes in the center."

Dr. Hardy smiled and placed a can of Natural Light beer in the middle of the candle formation. "This should flush him out!"

"I have this rag that I wiped up the bloodstain with," said Buddy Moore. He held a white cloth, discolored with dark brown stains.

"Okay, good. Put it out there too," she directed. "Now, what objects seem to be involved by his visits, or hauntings?"

"Ah, the BP and pulse ox monitor," answered Alan. "Usually all sixes light up on the display."

"Fine. Can we have the monitor on during our session?"

"Absolutely," he replied eagerly, and reached up to activate the unit.

"Okay. The basis of Wicca is to summon and channel the forces of nature to achieve a desired outcome. We must all focus on communicating with the spirit of ... Oh, what's his name?"

"Greg Jackson," stated Lucy. "The asshole!"

"Okay, Greg Jackson. We will gather around the table, sitting on this bench and cot, and join hands to form a circle. This will help channel our psychic energies to reach the spirit of Greg Jackson. Do not break the ring of hands until we end the session. We'll take turns repeating the chant. Is everybody ready?"

Dr. Hardy looked about the group as each reservedly took a seat and nodded. He held Julie's hand with his right and Lucy's with his left. His heart swelled in his chest during the minute of silence before Julie closed her eyes and spoke. She called upon the forces of nature.

"Mother Earth, wind, water, and fire, we ask your help in finding a lost soul. We offer him these gifts of life into death. May Greg Jackson be guided by our light and visit us tonight."

She repeated the last phrase twice more before opening her eyes and nodding to Dr. Hardy.

"May Greg Jackson be guided by our light and visit us tonight," he repeated. Julie turned to Lucy, who continued to speak the phrase. The chant continued around the circle. Over and over the phrase was voiced, like a skip in an old record album, the repetitive drone creating a hypnotic air. Nothing unusual occurred during five cycles around the group. Then, as Lucy sleepily spoke in turn, there suddenly arose the sound of footsteps. *Clomp, clomp, clomp.* Her grip tightened on Dr. Hardy's hand, and her eyes widened when she heard this too-familiar sound. The monitor display suddenly flashed with all sixes. There was a distinct *pfisst* sound, like the opening of a can of soda. All eyes were drawn to the beer, but it appeared undisturbed. The interior lights flickered in the ambulance and the monitor display changed. The green digits flashed in a new pattern: ALd/ONE. The display pulsed brightly at first, illuminating the ambulance with an eerie glow. It then grew dimmer with each pulse, until fading out completely.

Buddy Moore was the first to break the circle, leaping out of the side door. Julie's eyes sparkled with excitement and she exclaimed, "It's him! It's Greg Jackson!"

"I believe it is!" said Dr. Hardy.

"Oh, yeah!" Alan agreed. "Now, I think I could use that beer!" As Julie blew out the candles of positive energy, he grabbed the can. He froze and his face went white. "It's empty!" he exclaimed, astonished.

"Let me see that," said Hardy skeptically. He seized the can, still sealed tight, but light as a feather. The beer was really gone. "Holy shit! It is!"

"The rag," noted Lucy. "Look at it!"

The wash cloth was as white as if freshly laundered. Alan picked it up and spread it over his hands.

"The bloodstains are gone," he said. He called out through the still-open side door. "Buddy! Hey, Buddy! You forgot your rag!" Stepping out into the garage bay, he discovered that Buddy had fled the scene.

"The display," Hardy said to Julie, "do you have any idea what it might mean?"

"I'm not certain, but it looked like the digital spelling of A-L-D-O-N-E, or *all done*. Maybe, if that's right, his conflict may be *all done* now. Does that make sense?"

"I certainly hope so!" He then heard Alan's voice calling from outside.

"Buddy! Come on back, Buddy! It's all over."

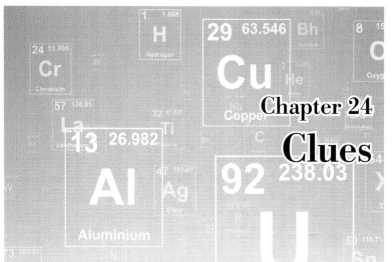

The second-year results of the home radon testing project were in. James Callahan had collected the readings and placed each one at the appropriate student's desk. When his Science 101 class convened, he addressed the students.

"I've placed each of your radon sample readings at your desks along with a map. The colored dots on the maps show last year's results. The readings are recorded in picocuries per liter and the range groups corresponding to each color are listed—from less than 1 pCi/L as white, up to greater than 4, which is red. I want you each to go over to the state map on the bulletin board and place the colored pin of your reading level at the location of your home."

The chaotic cluster of teenagers was flavored by chattering.

"Are these sewing pins?"

"Blindfold Macon, turn him around three times, and give him his pin."

"Maybe I don't get the point."

"Wow! You live out in the sticks!"

As the classmates returned to their seats, the commotion settled and Callahan began speaking again.

"Now, what would be the hypothesis for this study?" Several hands were raised. "Anna," he called.

"Do radon levels vary at different locations?" Anna responded.

"Yes. In other words, are there regional differences in radon levels in Southside Virginia?" While he spoke, he looked over at the map and stopped cold. He was shocked to see orange and, now, red pins! Last year had found only two orange pins and no reds. He suppressed his urge to immediately sit down and calculate the statistics. Were these findings real? Was this variation of scientific significance?

Somehow, he fumbled his way through the day's lesson material. Then he lost no time embarking on his mathematical mission. Using his scientific calculator, he ran the chi-square data analysis. Waiting for the students to reach the project's conclusion was precluded by his driving curiosity. The probability p value result was 0.08, confirming his suspicions. The odds of these variations being only from randomness were 8 percent or 92 percent chance of a true difference. He looked up from his desk, pondering the meaning of these results. Staring at the dotted map, his eyes drifted over to the geological map, still on display beside the bulletin board.

"Hmm," he thought aloud. "I wonder if there is any relationship here?" He walked over to the wall to scrutinize the map.

D etective Duffer met with Mark McClain, who was gathering data for his weekly police report. Duffer shared the ME's office COF analysis with him.

"Wasabi?" said Mark.

"Yeah. Have you heard of it?" asked Duffer.

"Well, yeah. I had some once while at college in Richmond. It's used with sushi. It's really hot! Like horseradish."

"Do you know where you can get it around here?"

"Not hardly. It's an imported delicacy. Most Japanese restaurants just substitute a mixture of horseradish and hot mustard. Hey! They did have a guest sushi chef at Kahill's last month. *The News Progress* ran an ad for him. He might have brought some wasabi."

"Really? Would it have been the last week of August?"

"That sounds about right," said McClain.

Detective Duffer paid Kahill's a morning visit before the lunch crowd started. He met with Johnny, the restaurant's manager, a well-groomed young man with short, light brown hair.

"Johnny, I'm investigating a death and tracking down some clues that have turned up. I was hoping you could help me with some details."

"Sure, Detective," said Johnny. "I'll be glad to help in any way that I can."

"Well, the main questions I have center around your visiting sushi chef."

"Oh, Todeshi? Yeah, what about him?"

"Do you know if he served wasabi here?"

"I think so. Let me check his menu. Come back into my office."

They walked through the edge of the kitchen to reach the modest business office. Johnny sat at his desk and began typing on his computer.

"Hmm... Let's see. Yep. Wasabi was on the sushi menu."

"Great! Now, would you happen to have a record of wasabi customers on Friday, August 27?"

"If they paid cash, no. But 90 percent of our sales are by check or charge. It'll take a few minutes." He stepped through the office door into the kitchen and called, "Hey, Steve. Get Detective Duffer a sweet tea, okay?"

"Sure," replied Steve.

"Thanks!" Then, turning back to Duffer, he said, "I'll need to pull our register sales records. Have a seat."

When Johnny returned to his office, the detective was comfortable, holding a half-empty glass of tea.

"Good tea," said Duffer. "Thanks."

"No problem. You're in luck. We had twenty-six sushi orders that night, but only six ordered wasabi. I have a list of their names for you." He held out a sheet of paper to Duffer. "I can release names of customers, but any credit card information is protected."

"Yeah, sure. I'll issue a warrant for that if needed. Thanks so much for your help. And thanks again for the tea."

The following day, Carl Wilborn walked into Duffer's office. He said, "I've checked out the wasabi list we got. Four customers were locals and they have good alibis. The others were transients. One from the Baltimore area and the other from Roanoke. I haven't contacted them yet."

"Good," said Duffer. "The suicide note was not handwritten. It was typed up on his computer. With the COF analysis finding this wasabi and Brut deodorant, it means there was someone else there. It could have been staged suicide."

"Yeah, I see. I'll see what I can find on the other two."

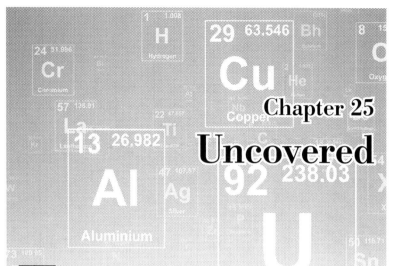

Chapter 25
Uncovered

The colorful autumn foliage metamorphosis was waning by the first week of November. A brisk freshness replaced the sultry summer air. The season's local high school football games had consumed Mark McClain's Friday evenings. His work was compounded by Mecklenburg County having two small high schools, instead of the single county school found in most rural Virginia counties. This forced Mark to select which game to attend. The team playing at home usually became his default choice. This week, both squads had away games slated, so he picked the game closer to Vanessa—Bluestone at Randolph Henry in Charlotte Courthouse. He left the office early to surprise Vanessa at the SVCC campus. With his face all agrin, he found her in the teachers' lounge.

Vanessa was looking over the shoulder of James Callahan, who was intensely focused on his laptop.

"You see these red spots?" he said enthusiastically. "They are high radon readings! This is new since last year's testing!"

"What's that mean?" she asked. Looking up, she suddenly noticed Mark. "Mark! Hi! James is showing me some new research data."

"Oh?" Mark dismissed a glimmer of jealousy. He was ever vigilant in search of newsworthy stories. "What's it about?"

"Well," Callahan explained, "my students have sampled their home radon levels for the past two years. This year, there was a significant rise in the levels in northeastern Harrison County."

"Oh," said Mark. "So, what *does* that mean?" Vanessa nudged him playfully for stealing her line.

"That's the million-dollar question," answered James Callahan. "I've got a theory. I compared our distribution pattern to the state geological map. There's a belt of shale stone rock running along the foothills of the Blue Ridge Mountains. This is a type of rock that may contain high concentrations of uranium ore. Radon is a radioactive gas, which is one of uranium's breakdown products. I was wondering if the earthquake two months ago caused some cracking that released some embedded uranium."

Vanessa looked from James to Mark. She appeared ashen, her dark complexion becoming pale.

"Well," she said hesitantly, "they have done some exploratory drilling for uranium in Harrison County."

"I wouldn't think such a limited level of environmental violation would free up any significant amounts of uranium," Callahan said.

"What if they went beyond the permitted drillings?" Mark posed. Vanessa was silent and appeared ill, as if her life humors were drained from her.

"They surely have regulations and monitor that stuff," said Callahan.

"Yeah. I guess so," Mark responded mechanically. He touched Vanessa's arm, reassuring himself she was indeed alive and well. "You ready for some Bluestone football?"

"Yeah, sure." Her response was weak.

"How about you riding with me to the game, baby? That way we can talk."

"Okay, Mark." She grabbed her coat from the hanger and walked out beside Mark.

"See you later, James," Mark said. "Maybe I'll call you next week and look into this further. Okay?"

"Yeah, sure. You two have fun."

As Mark drove off from the campus, Vanessa was still distant.

"Okay, Vanessa. What's wrong? Did something happen back there?"

"No." She remained withdrawn.

"So, are you and James... like... together?" He had to ask. He had not been suspicious of them before, but her behavior was so unusual.

"Oh, no!" she said weakly. "Nothing like that." She touched his thigh reassuringly.

"O... kay."

"Well, it's like this. I feel like a hypocrite, and I'm ashamed."

"About what?"

"Dixie Prospecting, the mining company."

"The ads you bring me to run? I've kinda wondered what was up with that. But, I didn't want to miss seeing you." She had seemed much the environmentalist type when he met her at the ethanol plant forum. To post ads for the uranium mining wannabe company had been out of character for her.

"I work for them, supposedly in marketing. But it's more than that." She had a serious, sheepish look.

"What do you mean?" Mark wondered if maybe they should have taken separate cars to the game.

"They've had me monitor the community's opinion on uranium mining. They even had me join the Association to Preserve Mecklenburg, which is a good organization anyway. I've been doing their recon." Her tone was somber.

"So, you're a spy?" Mark surmised.

"Well, it sounds worse when you say it like that. But... yes."

"So where *do* you stand on uranium mining in Virginia?"

"It scares me."

"Me, too," he replied, "at gargantuan levels!"

She sounded sincere to him. Mark wanted to believe her and that, maybe, she had come clean. This disappointment cast a dark shadow on their sizzling relationship.

"I can't take back what I've done. I can definitely quit and walk away from them!"

"Okay, but let's think about this some. Maybe we can use it somehow." He knew that some companies had executives who bought shares of competitors' stock to keep informed of the business endeavors. At least for now, he just wanted to break the intensity. "How about a football game? You up for it?" He squeezed her thigh firmly.

She smiled at Mark. "You bet!"

The game was a welcome distraction for them, revisiting a familiar, positive shared activity. Under the field lights, walking the sidelines together, they followed the action on the field. He felt hopeful that their relationship would survive. Even Bluestone High School showed promise, having entered the contest with a three-and-five record and two games remaining. They managed a win with a score of 22-18 and had a chance for an even season if their final game allowed.

On the drive back to the Keysville campus, Mark resumed their pregame discussion. "I've been thinking, Vanessa. We could use your association with Dixie Prospecting to investigate them."

"Oh, yeah? What do you mean?"

"Do you think you could get me into their drill site?"

"Hmm. I guess I could say you were doing a story, inspired by their ads. It could be like giving them a chance to sell themselves," she proposed.

"Yeah! That might work!" He smiled at her approvingly. "Of course, I won't know what I'd be looking for."

"I can ask James. He might give us some insight to work with."

"Yeah. I say we sleep on it tonight." Mark raised his eyebrows mischievously.

"Okay. Your place is closer, though."

"Deal!"

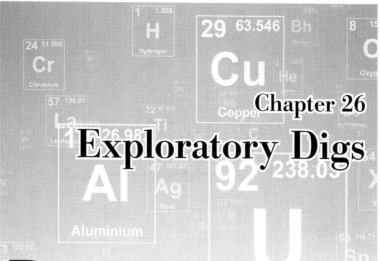

Chapter 26

Exploratory Digs

Detective Duffer met with Carl Wilborn to hear an update on his findings in the Porterman hanging investigation. He reported that the transient from the Baltimore area had continued driving south after eating at Kahill's. The motel check-in time in Durham, North Carolina, verified his itinerary time line.

"He had no time to have committed a murder and staged a suicide. Also, I could find no connection between him and the victim," stated Wilborn.

"Okay," said Duffer, somewhat discouraged.

"But," said Wilborn, "the other diner works for the same company as the decedent!"

"Oh, really?"

"Yep! Neal Hooker." Mark handed him a print of Hooker's DMV photo. "Both are employed by Dixie Prospecting, based in Roanoke. Porterman was a truck driver who worked out of this area. Hooker is in marketing. He allegedly had a meeting with our county business bureau that afternoon and claims to have driven home after eating."

"Can anyone verify that?"

"Not really. He did indeed attend that meeting, but he lives alone in Roanoke."

"That's still no suspicion or evidence that he would kill a co-worker. And, a truck driver? It doesn't seem there would be a motive. But it's worth talking to him."

"Should we have him brought in?"

"No. We don't have anything strong enough to justify that. He's just a person of interest for now."

Later, Detective Duffer happened to be in Clarksville when he heard a radio call go out. There was a nearby traffic wreck where a truck had overturned and he recognized the isolated location on Townsville Road. It was near the suicide scene he had investigated earlier in the year. He thought he'd just drive on down to the area cited. Technically, the Virginia state police and a county deputy were working the case. There were two trucks, one lying on its right side, and the other parked on the shoulder farther down. The vehicles both sported a circular gold emblem with blue DP letters. From the rear of the cargo area of the overturned truck there oozed a grayish, mud-like substance.

"Hey! Don't get close to that spill!" called out the state trooper. "We haven't verified its contents yet!"

"Okay. I'm Detective Duffer. Anything I can do to help out?"

"Well, I'm talking to the driver. You can get a statement from the other truck driver, if you like. See if he knows anything useful."

"Sure. I'll do it," Duffer answered.

"Thanks!"

Duffer met with the other driver at his upright truck. He carried a clipboard with him for notations. As he studied Alex Jeffers's drivers permit and CDL certificate, he said, "So, Mr. Jeffers, what can you tell me about the wreck?"

Mr. Jeffers was a short-statured, middle-aged man with a balding head. "Well, officer, Tim is a new driver. I've run this route for years and the pothole back there has just gotten bigger. Marvin and me knew to slow down along here. Tim's just young and inexperienced. He didn't do anything wrong. That hole's just a highway hazard!"

"I see, sure. So what happened to your regular driver?"

"Marvin? They say he hung himself, but I don't know for sure."

"Was he Marvin Porterman?" asked Duffer, now a little excited.

"Yeah, Porterman. You've heard of him?"

"Well, yeah. I'm still investigating his death." Maybe this driver has some information about Porterman that would help. "When we're done here, I'd like to discuss your working with Porterman. Anything you know about him may help me."

"Okay. Sure. He was a solid worker."

M ark met Vanessa at Southside Virginia Community College to start their trip. Wednesdays were her short days at the college, so she scheduled her meeting with Dixie Prospecting's regional manager, Mr. Snelling, for that afternoon.

"We can use my car," Vanessa suggested. "It is a job-related meeting for me."

"Okay," said Mark. He gathered his camera, clipboard, and file folder before getting into the passenger side of her red Honda Civic.

"What's with the file?" asked Vanessa, as they pulled onto the highway.

"Oh, odds and ends. Bits of information on the Bentley case, the uranium mining moratorium."

"Am I in your file?"

"No. My espionage files are classified," he responded with a serious tone.

"Well, just remember, paper boy, you're riding in the spy's car and it may have an ejection seat!"

On their arrival they encountered an eight-foot-high chain link fence outlining the entrance with the large, sliding gate spread open. Mark felt the Dixie Prospecting's drill site was surprisingly well developed. The business office was a single-story steel building with a stone façade covering the lower third. Off to the left rear, there was an enormous warehouse-like structure with three large garage-type doors. Two gray trucks with DP logos were parked outside the building. Vanessa pulled up to the office parking area. There was an aerial map mounted on the back wall with red dots scattered over it. The receptionist directed them to Walter Snelling's office.

"Ms. Foster," Mr. Snelling said, smiling sincerely. "It's good to see you again!"

"Yes," she said. "Mr. Snelling, this is the reporter from *The News Progress*, Mark McClain. He's set all of your ads for the paper."

"Oh? Well, thank you, Mr. McClain." He approached and shook hands.

"Sure, and thank you for your ads. It's good to meet you, sir."

"And this is Neal Hooker, our marketing director." He gestured to the dark-skinned man in a gray business suit.

"Good day, Mr. McClain, Ms. Foster," Hooker said most cordially.

Mark smiled but froze momentarily. His mind registered that this tall, black man fit the description of a suspect in his file.

"Good afternoon," came Mark's forced response.

"So, I hear you're doing an article on uranium mining," Hooker said.

"Yes, he is," said Vanessa.

"Ah… absolutely," Mark concurred, remembering their cover.

"Well, I have the safety research I'd like to share with you."

"Oh, sure. I'd like to see it," Mark said with feigned eagerness.

Neal Hooker showed them his lobbying posters, some brochures, and copies of research articles, explaining how the hazardous byproducts could cause no real threat. "The government labels this TENORM, an acronym for Technologically Enhanced Naturally Occurring Radioactive Materials. The US Environmental Protection Agency maintains a database on the four thousand mines currently producing uranium. They work to assure the safety of the public and the environment."

"Does the EPA work with laws regarding uranium mining?" asked Mark, as he steadily recorded notes.

"Well, yes, although they usually extend their authority to other state or federal agencies. There are fourteen states in the western United States with significantly rich uranium ore deposits."

"So why the interest here in Virginia?"

"Why? Only because it's one of the largest sources of uranium in the world!"

The four of them traveled by golf cart to the large building. As they approached, they met the two cargo trucks that were en route to the highway. Mr. Hooker led the party inside where a large truck was parked. An angular, metal-trussed beam stretched from atop the cab out to the rear.

"This is a drill truck, somewhat like a well-drilling rig. We take it to each drill site."

Mark began taking some pictures while Vanessa drifted about, studying the vehicle.

"You might want a shot from this angle, Mark," she suggested.

"Okay. I'll see," Mark responded as he walked over.

Vanessa looked at him, rolling her eyes to her left and nodding with her head. "See what I mean?"

Mark peered off behind her in the indicated direction. There were numerous industrial drums stacked some distance past the truck.

"Yeah, I see now," he said. He zoomed his camera in on the canisters and kept photographing. He also took some shots of Neal Hooker. Something was odd here or maybe he was just paranoid by being around a uranium bed. "Oh, Mr. Hooker?"

"Yes?" answered Neal.

"Do the workers wear radiation suits when they're out drilling?"

"Sometimes the ones on the drill equipment do. Uranium ore isn't that concentrated. Most rock has less than ten parts per million. A rich field like this one may have twenty times that! We hope so, anyway."

Mark looked at Vanessa with raised eyebrows and a poker face.

The following day, Mark returned to SVCC campus to review his photos with Vanessa and James Callahan. James enthusiastically scrutinized every picture Mark displayed on his laptop screen. The shots of the barrels in the background of the drill truck seemed to capture his interest.

"Hey, Mark," said James. "Did you get a closer view of those?" He pointed at the barrels.

"I'll zoom it in," said Mark. As the image enlarged, the labeling on the canisters became legible.

"Caustic: alkaline," Callahan read aloud. "Hmm."

"What's that mean?" Vanessa asked excitedly.

"Well, it's odd to see that stocked at a site for exploratory drilling."

"What's it used for?" inquired Mark.

"Alkaline leaching!" Callahan exclaimed.

"Leaching?" said Vanessa.

"Yeah. There are basically three mining techniques used for uranium: underground mining, which is only practical for large, shallow deposits; open pit mining, once the standard in the United States and Australia; and in situ leaching. In leach mining, acid or alkaline solutions are piped down bored shafts and pumped up nearby shafts. The chemicals release uranium from the rock and the resulting slurry is highly concentrated."

"So, do you think they might be *mining* the exploratory site?" asked Mark.

"They could be." They each mulled the gravity of this scenario for a moment. Callahan concluded, "I need to see this for myself. I'm going there Saturday morning!"

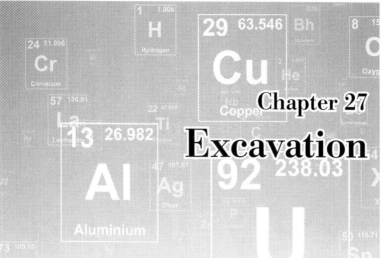

Chapter 27

Excavation

Detectives Duffer and Wilborn met with Alex Jeffers at the sheriff's office in Boydton. Mr. Jeffers appeared comfortable in a plaid flannel shirt and jeans. They sat at a Formica-topped table in the meeting room. Duffer began the interview.

"So, Mr. Jeffers, what did you feel was unusual about Marvin Porterman's suicide?"

"Well, Marvin was a good driver for DP. He was loyal to the company. A few months ago there was an incident on the job. Since that time, he was real stressed, not resting well, nervous-like."

"What did this incident involve?" probed Duffer.

"It's kinda creepy. We often made night runs and would take a lunch break on the road. So, about 4 a.m. one night, we stopped at a park on the lake. There was only one car in the parking lot, but no one was around. We were talking about our company's business doings, kinda private stuff. Then we heard someone at the car. Marvin thought he might have been listening to us, and he got scared. He went over to the man and yelled out, 'Hey, you! What're you doing here?' The man freaked out and ran off down the path. It was dark and Marvin ran after him with a flashlight."

"So, what happened then?"

"Marvin wasn't sure. He came back to the truck, pale as a ghost. He said he heard splashing in the lake and the man cried out for help. In the thick bushes and the dark, he couldn't see the man. He was afraid the man drowned! And he blamed himself for it!"

"Where was this lake site you were at?" inquired Duffer, with a keen interest now.

"Just off Townsville Road. Old Soudan Park." Duffer's suspicion was confirmed. That was the mysterious Lamont Stillman drowning.

"What private business stuff had you been discussing?" Carl Wilborn asked.

Mr. Jeffers lowered his head, pausing before breaking his confidentiality. "Our trucks ... they carry cans of drilling waste from the Harrison site to the Townsville mine. The workers unload it wearing radiation suits."

"Your manifest list says rock tailings and wash water," Duffer stated.

"Yeah, right!" Jeffers responded sarcastically. "We were talking, sort of joking, about hauling uranium in our trucks. If that got out, we could lose our jobs! The company could go under!"

"So," asked Duffer, "how did Marvin deal with this?"

"Well, he told me he went to see Mr. Snelling. Snelling told him everything was all right. But he still worried about it. Then, I heard he was hung." He shook his head sympathetically. The detectives' gazes met, suspiciously.

James Callahan had readily agreed to meet Mark McClain in Drakes Branch that Saturday morning. It was opening day of deer season, so he had selected hunting garb as a disguise. A stray hunter lurking about the perimeter might be less alarming to DP workers than a snoop.

"Whoa! What's up, Rambo?" Mark said when they met. "Are you planning a hunt?"

"Well, yeah, I guess I am. I'm hunting for a snake," he replied with a smirk.

"All right. Get in, Professor." As they rode off, Mark reviewed the DP site layout with him. "Remember, the complex is surrounded by a chain link fence, at least out front. I'm not sure if it runs the entire circumference or not."

"Okay." Callahan unrolled his Google Map satellite image map. The evening before, he had scouted his objective. He pointed to the road leading to the drilling location. "I'm hoping you can let me out about here. That way, I shouldn't be visible from the front gate."

"Okay," Mark agreed.

"If they find you, you can just say you came back for some follow-up photos or something."

"Yeah, that should work."

As they neared the DP property, Mark slowed down. "How about here?" he asked.

"Okay. Fine." Callahan took his book-bag-sized utility pack and scampered off the roadside. "Give me ninety minutes," he called back.

"Roger!"

He followed the border for about three hundred yards, at which point the chain links ended. The fence then became an open-wired, livestock-type barrier that continued around the property. So far, he had identified the office building and the larger, commercial-sized structure. A lone figure traveled between the two on a utility vehicle. Two cargo trucks were parked in front. No other workers appeared to be on duty this weekend. A road trailed off from behind the buildings. Callahan had to see where it led, hopefully to a drill site.

His foray continued for about half a mile until he spotted a maze of pipes. He took some pictures, but at this distance, he couldn't ascertain a pattern or purpose of the assembly. *I've got to get a closer look*, he thought. He climbed across the fence, checked for any observers, and then proceeded to the network of pipes.

From the edge of the spread, he began studying the system. Most of the pipes were about six inches in diameter and colored white or gray. The separate colored pipes converged into a larger, thirty-six-inch-diameter main of the same color. The white and gray main lines fed into individual machine blocks. Callahan guessed these were pump housings. The pipes spidered outward with the whites leading to the farthest locations, each ending about fifty yards apart. Another row of gray pipes were similarly spaced, positioned about fifty yards closer, flanked by an additional row of white pipes even nearer. The darker pump station appeared to dump into a concrete-lined drain pond, filled with grayish, tan, muddy fluid. The other pump house had a twelve foot tall tank mounted beside it.

Callahan took photos but paused frequently as he assimilated the workings of such a setup. Just in case, he pulled out his smartphone and took pictures of the two pump stations. He sent them to Mark. From the large tank, he rationalized, something must be pumped into the ground. The other had orange, OSHA radioactivity warning emblems painted on its sides. It must be extracting some fluid, the effluent, being dumped into the holding pool.

"In situ leaching!" he said aloud. Then he heard a humming, machine-type noise. It didn't sound like hydraulic pumping. He moved over to the white pump station to investigate the sound.

"Hey! You!" someone cried out. "This is a restricted area!" Callahan saw a uniformed man riding a four-wheeled work vehicle. His heart began racing. He turned, leapt over the large conduit, and set out for the fence. His escape was impeded by his hurdling across the pipe network. "Halt! You're trespassing!" He now wished he'd included a hunting rifle in his uniform.

He had reached a full sprint when the security officer overtook him. The vehicle halted abruptly across his path and the officer aimed a handgun at him. "I said, stop!" commanded the driver.

Callahan slowly raised his hands. "I'm sorry," he panted. "I was just hunting... and..." He searched for words. "My dog came over here and I was..."

"Save it, bud. Get in the Mule."

The security officer was a stout black man with a nonathletic physique. Had they both been on foot, Callahan was sure he would have eluded apprehension. The officer stood beside the vehicle and called in to report this development.

"Yes, sir. No problem," he said, and then turned back to Callahan. "I'll need your cell phone and camera," he demanded. Stripped of his electronics, Callahan was transported to the main building. There he was directed to a windowless utility room and shoved inside. "Wait here, for now," the officer said to him. "I'll be back in a few minutes." The door closed and he heard the click of a deadbolt.

Chapter 28
Trespassing

After the interview with Mr. Jeffers, Duffer placed a call to the Virginia DMME office in Charlottesville. He had some more questions for the late Phil Bentley's supervisor.

"Yes, Detective Duffer. I hope this call is under better circumstances than our last one."

"Well, it's just a follow-up to our previous discussion. I have a few more questions," Duffer began.

"Sure. I'll help any way I can."

"You said Bentley had filed his report on the Dixie Prospecting site visit on April 19."

"Right. He did."

"Okay. Now, was everything in order with that inspection?"

"Yes. They passed with flying colors. Why?"

"Well, I have suspicions that they may be moving radioactive waste. Could Bentley have overlooked something?"

"There was something unusual," said the supervisor. "I didn't make much of it at the time. Bentley always collected his notes in the field and prepared his reports here at the office. That report was sent electronically, from his laptop. He had never submitted one that way before."

"How would I determine if there were unauthorized activities going on there?" asked Duffer.

"I could send another inspector out there. Do you think we need to do that?"

"Yes. I think we do," stated Duffer flatly.

Callahan figured it had been over two hours since Mark had dropped him off on his mission. His phone had indicated that the pictures he had sent Mark had been successfully transmitted. That had been his last communication. He wondered if Mark understood what they showed. Moreover, he imagined Mark was probably becoming quite concerned by now. What if they had caught him as well?

He analyzed every item inside the locked room, hoping to discover an escape tool. His inventory included: a mop, a broom, a bottle of all-purpose cleaner, an oil can, trash bags. He picked up the broom and made sweeps and jabs in the air as if it were a sword. He recalled the security officer's pistol and abandoned this plan. The door hinge hubs were on the outside of the door and inaccessible. He resolved his fate to that of helpless waiting.

He estimated that forty-five minutes to an hour had passed before he heard footsteps on the concrete floor outside. As the lock opened, he faced the door and cautiously took two steps back. The door opened to reveal the security guard and another man in a business suit. He was a slender black man who appeared over six feet tall. The man looked sternly at him and spoke.

"Mr. Callahan, I'm sure you're aware that you were trespassing in a restricted area."

"Ah... yes, sir. I didn't mean to—"

"Just drop the bullshit! I'm Neal Hooker, from management of Dixie Prospecting. This is an exploratory drilling site. Our drilling and processing equipment can pose risks to the general public."

"Yes. I can see that now." *That's not all I see*, he thought, but he felt it prudent to hold his tongue.

"I've reviewed your photos, Mr. Callahan, and I'm concerned that you're stealing proprietary industry secrets. That's illegal!"

"I just thought that showing some mining operations would be of interest to the students in my science class. I never intended to violate any laws!" *You are the ones violating laws!* he wanted to say.

"Nonetheless, if we seek to prosecute you, we'll have to show this information to the court. It would then be public. That, too, would not be in our best interest. You seem to leave me little choice."

"It's okay," said Callahan. "I can delete those pictures! No problem!"

"I think you know that there is a problem, even more serious." His eyes were cold and stern. "The answer may be for me to delete you!" He nodded to the security guard who promptly walked off. There arose a hollow-sounding rattle, like metal rolling on the floor. The security guard appeared behind Mr. Hooker, pushing an empty steel drum that he then turned upright. The canister was labeled "Danger— Caustic Alkaline" with a white-and-black diamond-shaped emblem. "Mr. Callahan, as a science teacher, you may be aware of what effect sodium hydroxide has on the human body."

"Yes. Liquifactive necrosis," he responded flatly.

"Exactly! It melts all body tissue off the bones. There's no incriminating evidence left!"

Callahan had taken on more than he had expected. He realized that Hooker was threatening a Mafioso-style execution. His heart sank and knees weakened.

"Why? Why all this trouble?"

"Do you have any idea of the value of this uranium field?" Hooker asked.

"I've read about six to eight billion or so," Callahan reported.

"Close. Try twelve billion dollars! For this amount, you can expect us to use extreme measures." He stepped aside and the guard entered with a plastic draw-clamp fastener.

"Gimme your hands," he ordered.

Callahan held his hands out, resolved now that his death was eminent. In desperation, he made a low dive forward, scampering between the legs of his captors. He crawled back onto his feet as the guard yelled.

"Stop! I'll shoot!" He drew his pistol and took aim.

"Police! Drop your weapon!" cried a new voice.

Callahan looked around with a start. "What?" he said weakly. A state trooper and two county police had three 9 mm sidearms aimed at the guard.

"Put your hands on your heads and come forward," commanded the state policeman. The surprised guard and Neal Hooker complied with the orders. Detective Duffer was one of the county lawmen. He stepped over to Neal Hooker and began handcuffing his wrists.

"Mr. Hooker, you're under arrest for the murders of Phil Bentley and Marvin Porterman," Duffer said with an element of pride. The Harrison police officer read them both their rights as he cuffed the security guard, the accessory.

"This is an outrage!" Hooker cried. "I'll have your badges for accusing me of these bogus charges!"

"Maybe you haven't heard about pulling evidence out of thin air," Duffer responded with a sarcastic smile. Sniffing the air, he added, "I'm pretty sure I can detect a scent of Brut!" He turned to Callahan as the other lawmen led Hooker and the guard off. "Are you okay, Mr. Callahan?"

"Yeah, now. Just a little shaken up." He continued to speak to the detective. "I think there's some more deception here that may interest you as well."

"The drilling sites?"

"Yeah! I think they may be illegally leaching uranium! How'd you know?"

"Mark McClain forwarded me your photos when he reported you as missing in action. The Virginia DMME is on the way here now to investigate. You took a big risk here, you know?"

"Yeah. I think they were going to shove me in a barrel of lye!"

"It's alkaline hydrolysis, the green cremation. Yeah, I think Mr. Hooker is familiar with that process."

"So, where's Mark now?" asked Callahan.

"Battlefield reporting, James," came Mark's voice from off to the side. He lowered his camera from his face, exposing a broad grin. "A *News Progress* exclusive! Making headlines and saving the world!"

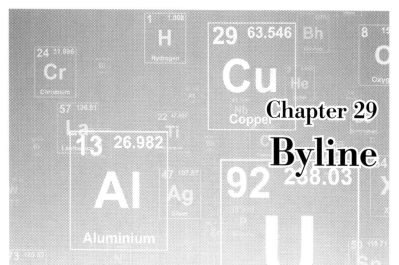

Chapter 29

Byline

Even though it was almost six in the morning, Mark McClain wasn't sleepy. The evening's sensual, sexual sojourn had placed him in a slumber of physical fulfillment. His mind, however, was as restless with excitement as a child on Christmas morning. Lying alongside him, Vanessa slept soundly. He kissed her gently on the cheek before getting out of bed. She sighed softly without moving.

Dressed only in his sweatpants, he poured himself a hot cup of coffee. He could read the headline of *The News Progress* that was on the kitchen table: Uranium Mining Officials Indicted. It was his story, front page, with photos! The *Richmond Leader* had even picked up his story. He sipped his coffee and chuckled a little.

"What's so funny?" asked Vanessa. She stood in the doorway wearing a pink bathrobe. The thin cotton robe hung open slightly in the front, teasingly covering her nudity. Drawing close, she put an arm around his waist and took his cup with the other hand. He felt her body's warmth as she took a sip of his coffee.

"Well, I was just thinking of the headline I wanted to use."

"What was it?"

"Uranium Ore Whores Busted," he said, grinning. Vanessa laughed and then kissed Mark fondly.

"So would that make me their pimp?"

"Yeah, I guess so. Oh, I've got something for you," he said.

"Oh, yeah? What?"

He produced a small box from a kitchen drawer and handed it to her. "Here," he said.

"What?" she said, still a bit surprised. She looked at him and then opened the box. A silver ring mounted with a princess-cut, translucent bluish stone gleamed from inside. She paused, as if contemplating the meaning.

"Don't worry. It's not an engagement ring!" Mark clarified. "It's just a memento of our adventures together, a token of my affection."

She planted a more passionate kiss on his lips, catalyzing an arousal response in Mark.

"Thank you! I love it!" she said seductively. "What type of stone is it?"

"It's kyanite," Mark said smiling. "I had it cut and mounted especially for you."

Vanessa put on her new jewel and let her robe fall open lasciviously. She turned back toward the bedroom and allowed her robe to slide off her back onto the floor behind her.

"I feel like celebrating," she said, over her shoulder, as she disappeared into the bedroom. Mark felt that way too!

At the Mecklenburg County sheriff's office, Detective Bruce Duffer laid down *The News Progress* edition he had just read. Carl Wilborn entered and asked Duffer, "So, where's this uranium they extracted?"

"I don't know. The DMME didn't find any stockpiled on the site, only some in the discharge ponds."

"Didn't the truck wreck have uranium cargo on board?" asked Wilborn.

"They said they were carrying drilling waste. But why would they carry this to Townsville?" Duffer queried.

"Well, what did the DMME say?"

"They are a Virginia state organization. North Carolina is

out of their jurisdiction." Duffer was more than a bit frustrated. Moving the ore across state lines had made it difficult to trace. "And the Nuclear Regulatory Commission doesn't regulate TENORM, Technologically Enhanced Naturally Occurring Radioactive Material."

"We should have some way to investigate this further. Shouldn't we?" asked Wilborn.

"I don't know. Maybe the EPA. I think they require having a complaint filed first."

"It could be too late by then!" Wilborn said.

"I'll look into that right away!"

Lucy Hardy brought her Monday newspaper into the office with the morning mail. The lead story wouldn't keep until lunch break.

"They raided the uranium site!" she announced. "Apparently, they had been mining uranium illegally!"

Dr. Hardy was at the pass-through counter, writing charts between patients. "Let me see that," he said. He studied the front page briefly. "It seems those unidentified bones were the key to the investigation! Hey, Lucy, isn't that a picture of James Callahan, Anna's teacher from the community college?"

Lucy took a second look and replied, "It sure is! What's he doing there?"

"I don't know. Read it and find out." He moved on to the next exam room. It wasn't until that evening that he realized the role his daughters' science projects played in the case and the magnitude of the environmental disaster that had been looming.

James Callahan walked into the dean's office at the John H. Daniel campus of SVCC. He was still riding the wake of his recent catapult into the spotlight. Maybe he could reap some extra research supplies.

"I've got a request for some more research equipment," he said as he handed his form to the secretary.

"Okay, Mr. Callahan," she said politely. She briefly perused the requisition and read aloud, "Radiation protection suit and a Geiger counter, right?"

"Yep!" Callahan responded with a scheming smile. He added, "Another *research* project." After all, twelve billion dollars was a lot of money!

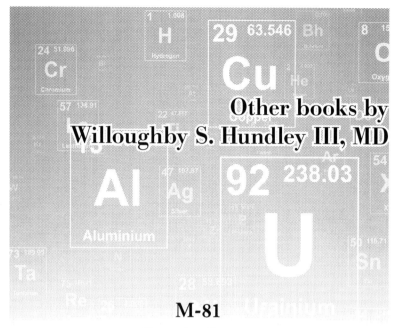

Other books by
Willoughby S. Hundley III, MD

M-81

Emerging Doctors

Ashes of Deception